D1622605

A
CANDLELIGHT REGENCY SPECIAL

CANDLELIGHT REGENCIES

216 A Gift of Violets, *Janette Radcliffe*
221 The Raven Sisters, *Dorothy Mack*
225 The Substitute Bride, *Dorothy Mack*
227 A Heart Too Proud, *Laura London*
232 The Captive Bride, *Lucy Phillips Stewart*
239 The Dancing Doll, *Janet Louise Roberts*
240 My Lady Mischief, *Janet Louise Roberts*
245 La Casa Dorada, *Janet Louise Roberts*
246 The Golden Thistle, *Janet Louise Roberts*
247 The First Waltz, *Janet Louise Roberts*
248 The Cardross Luck, *Janet Louise Roberts*
250 The Lady Rothschild, *Samantha Lester*
251 Bride of Chance, *Lucy Phillips Stewart*
253 The Impossible Ward, *Dorothy Mack*
255 The Bad Baron's Daughter, *Laura London*
257 The Chevalier's Lady, *Betty Hale Hyatt*
263 Moonlight Mist, *Laura London*
501 The Scandalous Season, *Nina Pykare*
505 The Bartered Bride, *Anne Hillary*
512 Bride of Torquay, *Lucy Phillips Stewart*
515 Manner of a Lady, *Cilla Whitmore*
521 Love's Captive, *Samantha Lester*
527 Kitty, *Jennie Tremaine*
530 Bride of a Stranger, *Lucy Phillips Stewart*
537 His Lordship's Landlady, *Cilla Whitmore*

The Sleeping Heiress

Phyllis Taylor Pianka

A CANDLELIGHT REGENCY SPECIAL

Published by
Dell Publishing Co., Inc.
1 Dag Hammarskjold Plaza
New York, New York 10017

Dell ® TM 681510, Dell Publishing Co., Inc.

ISBN: 0-440-17551-8

WFH

Printed in the United States of America
First printing—January 1980

The Sleeping Heiress

CHAPTER ONE

Amy Dorset hurried down the long dimly lit corridor of the main building at St. Catherine's Academy for Young Ladies. A slight frown creased her usually smooth forehead. It wasn't the ever present icy dampness of the high stone walls that troubled her; it was the summons she had received to report at once to the office of the headmistress. She smoothed the skirt of her gray-on-gray student's uniform and hastily tucked a copper-colored curl beneath her bonnet.

Whatever had she done now? It had been three years . . . *three years* since she had been reprimanded for unruly behavior. In all conscience she was at a loss to think of a single rule she had broken. She sighed heavily. It had taken the dour headmistress nine years to change her from a lively, spirited, happy child into a drab seventeen-year-old mouse. When her father, the Earl of Concord, enrolled her in the school at age five, he had left explicit orders that Amy was to lead a strictly disciplined life. The school had done its work well. She was a mere shadow of her old self; less noticeable even than the colorless, institutional furniture that repeated itself with monotonous dependability from classroom to social hall to dormitory.

Reaching the end of the hall, she tapped softly on the great mahogany doors, then, upon being bidden to enter, turned the knob and walked in. The first thing she noticed was the chandelier ablaze with candles, an occurrence unheard of this time of day. Amy bobbed a curtsy to Mrs. Dupreen, who looked strangely ill at ease behind the massive desk.

The headmistress pushed her spectacles down to the end of her nose as she stood and nervously came around the end of the desk. "Ah, here you are, my dear." Her smile was like thin ice on the garden pond in winter.

For the first time Amy noticed the visitor seated near the fireplace at the end of the room. She was a trim, white-haired woman, a good bit too short to be considered attractive, but there was a compelling quality about her that bespoke nobility. Her sprigged muslin traveling dress was partially covered by an exquisite blue brocade manteau piped in white brocade to match her muff.

Mrs. Dupreen took Amy by the arm. "Lady Charlotte Winford, may I present Lady Amy Dorset."

Amy was so shocked at having been introduced by her proper title that she forgot to curtsy until she was nudged by the headmistress. Lady Charlotte rose with practiced grace and came toward them, taking Amy's cold hands between her warm ones.

"Lady Amy, I'm sure you don't remember me but I was a good friend of your dear father." She motioned to the chairs. "May we sit down, please? I have something to tell you."

That was how this incredible day had begun. Now, six hours later, she and that remarkably small woman were riding side-by-side in the elegantly appointed State carriage belonging to her new guardian, the Duke of Haddonfield. She had left St. Catherine's for good, to make her home at Haddonfield Hall, the ancestral home of the Winford line since the reign of the Tudors.

Attempting to make herself invisible against the plush burgundy cushions that were embroidered with the Winford crest, Amy stole discreet glances at Lady Charlotte.

Her skin was thin to the point of being translucent, like the Dresden porcelain Amy remembered having seen as a child. Her eyes were a faded blue and should have lacked warmth but the tiny crinkles at the corners belied a cold disposition.

As if reading Amy's mind, Lady Charlotte tucked her hands into the white silk muff and smiled. "I know you must be terribly ill at ease of this sudden turn of events but I hope we are going to be friends."

Amy nodded. "Yes, ma'am. You said you knew my father. Were you with him when he . . . Did he suffer greatly?"

"No to both questions. Your father had just returned from a prolonged visit to the Continent. He had been home at his town house in London only a few hours when he was stricken, and died very quickly." A worry line creased the woman's forehead. "I'm sure you were told, Amy, that your father wished to be laid to rest without ceremony or undue fuss. His solicitor and the vicar were the only ones present."

Amy's face clouded. "My mother . . . was she told?"

"We thought it only proper that she be informed, although of course . . ." Lady Charlotte stopped in confusion.

Amy felt an immediate compassion for the woman's discomfort. She put her gloved hand on Charlotte's arm. "It's all right. I know a little of the circumstances surrounding my parents' unfor-

12

tunate marriage." She drew a deep breath. "I realize that my mother left my father and me when I was a child, to follow a career in the theatre. My father then petitioned Parliament and was granted a dissolution of the marriage. In return for relinquishing all rights to her child and her title my mother was given a monetary settlement of several thousand pounds." Amy paused reflectively. "I wonder, did she ask about me when they told her about my father?"

Charlotte's voice was thick with ill concealed emotion. "Oh, Amy, I'm sure she did. The solicitor would have told her that you would be well cared for. You must never think for one minute that your mother doesn't love you." She turned to stare through the carriage window. "There are some people in the world who seem to have a special calling. For your mother it was the stage. And neither husband nor child nor fortune could keep her from that calling. It's like something in the blood that cannot be denied."

"I wonder about her sometimes: what she is like and what she would think of me. I haven't seen her since I was five years old." Amy traced a seam in the cushion with the tip of her gloved finger.

In an obvious effort to change the subject Charlotte's tone brightened markedly. "We are going to be terribly busy these next few weeks. The first thing we must do is provide a new wardrobe for you. Do you like visiting the shops?"

"I've never been to the dressmakers. Saint Catherine's has always provided our uniforms so there was no need." She smiled shyly. "But I did enjoy the copies of the *Ladies' Quarterly* that Margaret Newcomb-White secretly brought to the dormitory."

"Then you will have a great treat in store for you and I shall enjoy it as much as you. I simply adore Bond Street."

"But surely it will be very expensive. Am I not penniless?"

A wave of color suffused Charlotte's face. "I think it best if Jason be the one to discuss financial arrangements with you. Suffice it to say that you will have enough money to easily afford a new wardrobe."

"Jason?" Amy was puzzled. "Did I perhaps misunderstand? I was under the impression that the duke was appointed my guardian. Is not Lord Jason Winford his son?"

"That is true, but the duke is rarely in residence at Haddonfield Hall. More often than not my brother is away on diplomatic missions for the Prince Regent. In his absence Jason is in charge of the duke's affairs." She let her gaze wander out of the window. "In truth the duke is aging rapidly. I fear it will not be long until Jason comes into the full responsibility that goes along with the title Duke of Winford. As it is now Jason manages

14

both Haddonfield Hall here in London and Winford Farms in the country."

For a while they were both content with their thoughts as they listened to the grate of the iron-rimmed coach wheels. Amy felt a growing apprehension as she watched the landscape change from open country with rolling wooded hills to cozy hamlets with the inevitable sparkling white church and bustling blacksmith shed in the village center. They passed groups of villagers returning from the marketplace, some with dogcarts still partly filled with baskets they had woven from osier rods cut from trees that were grown on their own farms.

The people were poorly dressed in comparison to Lady Winford's fine clothing. Amy felt uncomfortably aware of the stares of the curious who, after noticing the Winford crest emblazoned on the coach door, paused to get a closer look at the occupants. She was unused to being the object of curiosity. St. Catherine's had taught her that it was safer to stay in the background.

As they approached the city of London Amy leaned forward with eager anticipation. She had visited there three years ago with her father but it was the only time she had seen his rented town house on Great Swallow Street. She had loved the excitement of the city, what little she had seen, and now the thought that she might become a part of its social life was beyond belief.

As the carriage slowed to pass through a

street an urchin with a soot-blackened face grabbed hold of the door and pulled himself up to the window for a better look. The coachman turned around and ordered him off with a brandish of the whip. With progress slowed to a crawl one became instantly aware of the stench of the open sewers that flanked each side of the narrow street. It seemed to Amy that there were people everywhere. She wondered what attracted the crowds and Lady Charlotte pointed to the north.

"Most of them are coming from Covent Garden Market. You can get a better look as we pass Southampton Street. Look there to your right. Although most of it is behind the wall, you can catch a glimpse of the flower sellers' stalls and the fishmongers. There must be over two hundred different shops located within the market."

They rode along for a considerable distance with Amy wide-eyed at all there was to see, while Charlotte did her best to describe the many points of interest. As they passed Whitehall, St. James's Park, and then Green Park to Berkeley Street, Charlotte tapped on the windowsill.

"We will be there soon. To the left up ahead is Grosvenor Square where you will see the former residence of the Duchess of Kendal who used to be mistress to George the First. That is his statue in the center of the square. The duke's mansion is on the left after we cross North Audley Street." As the carriage turned onto Upper Brook Street

16

Charlotte pointed to a four-storied building of aged red brick. It was set cheek by jowl next to a half dozen mansions that also dated back to 1763 and were built on land which was part of the old Grosvenor estate that had come to Sir Thomas Grosvenor upon his marriage to twelve-year-old Mary Davies.

The house was imposing and it suddenly occurred to Amy that the master of the house might be equally as imposing. "Wh—what is he like, Lady Charlotte . . . Lord Jason, I mean?"

Charlotte smiled warmly. "I suppose some people think him rather stern. One certainly couldn't call him a dandy or a fop . . . even though the ladies of the beau monde tend to follow him like sheep after a ram. Jason takes the responsibility of nobility very seriously." She spread her hands. "But it's best that you see for yourself. Since I raised him after the death of his mother when he was little, my opinions are at best biased. I think you will like Jason. He held you on his lap once when you were a little baby. Did you know that?"

Amy clasped her hands together. "The truth is, Lady Charlotte, I know little of anything outside the school. I hardly even remember my father. We lived a cloistered life at Saint Catherine's."

Charlotte gathered her skirts around her and straighted her manteau as the carriage drew to a stop beneath a wide-pillared porte cochere that separated Haddonfield Hall from the adjoining

17

mansion. Amy felt a knot tighten in her stomach now that they had arrived. Charlotte looked pleased and a little excited at being home. There was a twinkle in her pale blue eyes. "I rather suspect, Amy, that your life is about to undergo quite a change."

Everything began to happen at once. A footman in blue livery hurried down the red-carpeted steps and opened the carriage door. Adjusting the folding steps, he handed Lady Charlotte down from the carriage and with a pleasant greeting, passed her on to another lackey who escorted her up the steps. Huge cast-iron torches lighted the entrance as if it were daytime. Amy, escorted by yet another footman, hurried to keep up with Charlotte.

Her first impression of the mansion was of spacious elegance. The glow of a hundred candles in chandeliers, which were raised to the vaulted ceiling by means of a satin rope, adequately lighted the entrance hall without disturbing the deep-set shadows at the sides of the room. The floor of blue-and-gold Italian marble tiles felt cool through the thin soles of her slippers. Centered in the foyer, a wide spiral staircase appeared to float, without obvious support, upward to the gallery of the second floor and beyond.

A footman assisted Amy in removing her traveling cloak and she was gratified to note that he showed not the slightest flicker of disdain at the shabbiness of her clothing. Charlotte took off her

18

gloves and handed them to a servant as she turned to Amy.

"Albert, the butler, tells me that Jason thought it might be best for you to rest this evening and refresh yourself from the journey. He will see you in the morning after you have had breakfast."

Amy felt disappointment mingled with relief. She anticipated the meeting with a certain amount of dread and yet she wanted to have done with it. Although Lord Jason was not her legal guardian, she would nevertheless be under his control until the duke returned. And hadn't Charlotte said that he was considered quite stern? She tried to put the thought out of her mind.

While the servants brought in the valise and portmanteau that contained her few possessions Amy followed Charlotte up the carpeted stairway to the second floor where she opened a door.

"You will have the corner suite adjoining mine," Charlotte said. "I hope you will find it comfortable. I chose most of the furnishings from what little I knew of you but, if you find them distasteful, you will have ample time to select what you like."

Amy was astonished at the room that was more than equal in size to the dormitory room at St. Catherine's where she and the others had slept. Her second impression was of softness, both in color and texture. The wool carpet that entirely covered the floor was as thick and luxuriant as the grass which grew in the shade of the summer-house at St. Catherine's. Its pale sage-green hue blended nicely with the delicate pink-blue-and-yellow-flowered draperies and bed canopy. In the adjoining sitting room a fire blazed in the hearth, revealing comfortable lounging chairs and a small tea table. Amy noticed that the table was set with a service of fine china bearing the Winford crest.

Charlotte looked a trifle ruffled when she saw Amy looking at the dishes. "Jason thought you might like to dine alone in your room this evening . . . what with all the excitement of your travels. Polly will bring a supper tray when she comes to unpack your things." She looked a bit hesitant. "Will you be all right, Amy?"

"Yes, yes of course, Lady Charlotte. And the room is perfect just the way it is. I can't find words to thank you."

She took Amy's hands in hers. "I just want you to be happy, my dear. I know this is all terribly new to you but I've been thinking about it for several weeks and looking forward to the opportunity to act as your chaperon. I know we are not related by blood, but if you like you may call me Aunt Charlotte."

"Thank you. I—I only hope I won't be a disappointment to you . . . or my guardian."

"Jason and his father are sure to be as enchanted with you as I am."

Amy had time to wonder about it later as she sat before the fire and dined on a tasty venison pie, jellied pigeon, and delicate pastries filled with scoops of apricot jam. Over the rim of the teacup she watched through the open door as Polly carefully unpacked and hung the drab uniforms in the spacious armoire. It was obvious that the plump, sandy-haired chambermaid was surprised by the miserly contents of the portmanteau.

"I'll be puttin' your stockings and things in the drawers, miss. Would you be likin' a bath or would you rather be off to bed?"

Amy suddenly longed for a warm soak. Her face brightened. "I would dearly love to have a bath if it's not too much trouble."

"No bother at all, miss." She opened a door that revealed a small bathing cubicle with another door, which Amy assumed led to Charlotte's bedchamber. A table piled high with woolly bath sheets and scented lotions stood next to a white enameled circular bathtub. "If you'll be wantin' it soon I'll fill the tub with 'ot water so it can be warmin' the room. Or if you feel the chill I could ask Albert to fetch it in by the fire."

"Please don't bother. It's fine where it is. I'll be ready as soon as I finish eating."

Later as she sat on the edge of the tub, and even later when she was lying between silken sheets in the high, canopied bed, Amy considered her new position in life. At one time she would have been thrilled by the exciting upswing of her fortunes, delighting in the wealth of new experiences and eager to see what lay in store. But the years of swift and sometimes unjust punishment had taught her to treasure the security of routine.

Now she was thrust into a situation where each passing moment was sure to bring unavoidable changes. She had learned to anticipate the moods of the headmistress. Would her new guardian be a sterner, less agreeable master?

The eiderdown suddenly felt like an unbearable weight on top of her. She felt the need of clean fresh air and slipped out of bed to swing the leaded window open an inch or two. It was cool for the first of May. The crisp air frosted her lungs as she breathed deeply.

Downstairs a lighted window in the central section of the mansion caught her attention. A tall, dark-haired man was leaning against the mantelpiece, apparently lost in thought as he stared into the fire. His thick, shoulder-length hair curled under slightly at the ends to rest against his jaw. As if summoned by her thoughts he turned and strode to the window where he rested his hands on each side of the window frame above his head. Standing as he was, spread-eagled and silhouetted against the light, he looked frighteningly like some giant bird of prey.

Amy dared not move lest his gaze be drawn upward to her window. She stood breathless, longing for the safety and comfort of her bed, but she was transfixed. There was no doubt in her mind that the man was Jason.

She let her breath out slowly, suddenly aware that she had forgotten to breathe. At that moment he lifted his head abruptly and stared straight at her window. Although she knew it had to be her imagination, she felt his glittering hawk's eyes penetrate the thin material of her cotton nightshift. With a squeal of alarm she whirled around and made a wild dive for the bed, pulling the cover over the top of her head.

What manner of man was he who could terrify her with a look? Dear heaven. How would she ever dare meet him face-to-face? The thought haunted her sleep and left traces of a restless night in the dark smudges beneath her eyes.

Polly woke her the next morning bearing a cheerful smile and a silver Sheffield breakfast tray, which she placed on the tea table near the fireplace. " 'Tis sorry I am to be wakin' you so early, miss, but the young master left orders to serve your breakfast. When you've done with it e'll be expectin' to see you in the library."

Amy forced a smile but could scarcely hide the shaking of her hands as she turned back the covers. In her mind's eye all she could see was that monstrous bird of prey hovering over her.

CHAPTER TWO

Amy quickly finished her morning ablutions and slipped into a clean, crisp gray-on-gray uniform. She smiled remembering Polly's embarrassment when the chambermaid had asked Amy what she wanted to wear. There was little choice. Her entire wardrobe consisted of the serviceable homespuns worn by all of the students.

"Never you fret, miss," Polly admonished. "You'll 'ave a fine time choosin' your new gowns. My! Think of all the decisions you'll 'ave to make!" She had said it as if it were something to look forward to with pleasure.

Amy regarded the prospect with apprehension. She had never been forced to make decisions concerning her personal care and the knowledge that she would soon be expected to use her own judgment was almost too much to cope with. She dawdled over her breakfast of kippered herring, fresh strawberries, and scones. Polly, bustling about as she set the room in order, cleared her throat, causing Amy to look up.

"If you'll pardon me, Lady Amy, I don't mean to rush you but 'is lordship can be a mite irritable when 'e's kept waitin'."

Amy sighed. "Thank you, Polly. I *was* hoping to put it off for a while but I might as well have done with it." She rose and smoothed her hair under her cap. "Lord Jason will be waiting for me in the library, will he not?"

"Yes, my lady. Turn left at the foot of the stairs and go through the double doorway. The footman will show you the way."

"Thank you, Polly." She paused at the door. "Lady Charlotte, has she risen yet?"

"Oh yes, miss. She is an early riser, that one. She'll be walkin' the dogs in 'yde Park about now, I expect."

Amy descended the stairs slowly. She had clung to the hope that Charlotte would be with her for this first meeting with her substitute guardian but Polly's words had deprived Amy of that slender straw. A footman standing near the main entrance doors came to attention and nodded a greeting. Another footman in the same blue-and-silver livery stood by the double doors. When Amy told

25

him that his grace was expecting her he reached a gloved hand to the great brass doorpull and motioned her to precede him down a dimly lit corridor flanked on each side by closed doors. Approaching a mahogany door, the footman stepped ahead of her, opened it, and announced, "Lady Amy Dorset, Your Grace."

Lord Jason Winford looked up from a stack of papers which were spread out on the table in front of him. As Amy curtsied in her best finishing school manner he stood and bowed gravely in response.

"Come in, Lady Amy," he said as he came around the table and motioned her to a chair near the bay windows. She sat down, lacing her fingers together on her lap, less from good manners than from an effort to keep them from shaking.

If only he would sit down, she thought. He was tall and most overpowering viewed from close up. A strong jawline was the predominant feature of his face. Dark, thick eyebrows and lashes framed clear blue eyes; not the penetrating hawk's eyes she had imagined last night. His voice was deep and resonant as he walked behind a Queen Anne chair and placed his hands firmly on the back.

"I am not quite sure where to begin, Lady Amy. No doubt Lady Charlotte has informed you of the pertinent details." Amy nodded as he continued. "It was your father's wish that you be under my father's guardianship until you marry or come of

26

age. In the absence of the duke, his authority in such matters falls to me. It was my decision, after some considerable persuasion from Lady Charlotte, that no good cause would be served by having you remain at Saint Catherine's Academy."

He stood erect and tugged at the jacket of his brown waistcoat, pulling it snugly against the top of his close-fitting, fawn-colored breeches. A nervous habit, Amy decided, and it made her feel good to think that he, too, might be uncomfortable. She ventured a question.

"I'm certain I shall ever be indebted to you for your kindness on my behalf, Lord Jason. Lady Charlotte tells me that I am not entirely without funds. Am I to understand, sir, that there will be enough of an inheritance to adequately repay you for my care? I would hate to be a financial as well as moral burden."

His face turned faintly pink and he ran a finger around the inside of his neckcloth as if it were too tight. Amy remembered that the question of her funds had caused a similar embarrassment to Lady Charlotte. He cleared his throat and turned toward the windows.

"I think it best that you not concern yourself about money for the present. I shall see that you are afforded a monthly allowance for your personal expenses in addition to a clothing allowance. Lady Charlotte, as your chaperon, will be able to advise you on what is suitable for a young lady in your position."

"Thank you, Lord Jason."

"With your permission I will call you Amy and ask that you address me as Jason."

At that moment Charlotte tapped on the door and strode into the room. Her orchard-green riding skirt swirled above mahogany kid leather hightop boots. "Good morning, everyone." She smiled brightly. "I had hoped to be back in time to introduce the two of you but the dogs missed their run yesterday and consequently took advantage of my generosity."

Jason smiled indulgently. "We were just discussing Amy's allowance and the fact that you would be able to help her choose a wardrobe."

"Oh, my, yes." Charlotte's white hair danced around her cheeks where it had escaped from her bonnet. "And we must make plans for a coming-out party."

Jason's voice cut through the air like a whip. "No, Charlotte. There is to be no formal debut. The Earl of Concord made it abundantly clear that he wanted his daughter to lead a quiet life."

"But surely the child will have to be introduced to Polite Society?" She smiled tolerantly. "I mean, Jason, dear, how else is a girl to make a suitable match unless she is presented to the beau monde?"

Jason was obviously unsettled as he strode back and forth across the richly furnished room. "I'm not saying that the girl must be kept in seclusion but I do draw the line at a formal coming out. Perhaps when Father returns he will feel differently but I cannot exceed my authority in this matter."

Charlotte's voice was sweet as honey. "Of course, you are right as usual, Jason. Instead of a formal presentation and a huge fete, we will have a series of intimate parties with a few possible suitors whom we select as guests. It is really the only way to approach it."

Jason started to protest but spread his hands in defeat. "Very well. I shall leave it to you."

"Fine. The first thing we shall do is select a wardrobe. I assume you have arranged for her clothing allowance?"

He nodded absently. "Pringle has his instructions. You may see him about the matter." Jason was so preoccupied that he hardly seemed aware when they left the room.

Amy had watched the little byplay with amusement. She saw the smug look on Charlotte's face and guessed correctly that her chaperon had won the concession she had wanted. She tucked Amy's hand under her arm as they climbed the stairs, her voice bubbling with excitement.

"My dear, we are going to have a marvelous time fitting you out. It has been years since this house has seen any laughter. Jason is far too serious for a man who has not yet reached thirty. He tries to fill his father's shoes but he is much too young to settle for an old man's pleasures."

When they reached the bedchamber Charlotte reached up and pulled off Amy's cap, letting the mass of burnished curls spill out. Charlotte clasped her hands in delight. "Oh, my! What a jolly good splash we are going to make in the London pond. It's my guess that before the summer is out the Carlton House set will wonder what hit them. Your name will be on the top of every society guest list for the next two years."

When Charlotte had gone to her own chambers to change Amy threw herself on the bed and blew out a loud sigh of relief. Never in all her life had she met two such dynamic and forceful personalities. Charlotte she adored, but Jason was another matter altogether. Where Charlotte was warm and endearing, Jason was cold and distant, although properly polite. She hadn't expected him to greet her with outstretched arms, but if he found any pleasure in her presence at Haddonfield Hall, he showed remarkable restraint in expressing it.

Just what Jason felt toward her was something to puzzle over. He seemed cool to the point of being remote. Was this typical of other men? Her previous experience with the male gender consisted mainly of a casual hello to the groundskeeper at school or a brief compliment from Herr Grimswold, her instructor on the pianoforte. Milli-

30

cent Greaver, on the other hand, had enjoyed several conversations with the young musician. Indeed the bubbly blond heiress had been held accountable for Herr Grimswold's dismissal from the staff when she had been discovered in his rooms without benefit of chaperon.

Amy ran to the full-length mirror and inspected herself closely. Her figure was more subdued than Millicent Greaver's voluptuous curves, and although gray uniforms did nothing for her pale skin, the bones in her face were good. There had to be some reason why men ignored her as if she were not there. One thing Amy knew for sure. Had it been Millicent whom Jason had interviewed in the library, he would have been less attentive to the papers on his desk.

Amy slowly replaced the cap over her curls. Lady Charlotte had a fine struggle ahead of her if she hoped to make her into a raging beauty. She straightened her shoulders and lifted her chin. If nothing else, her posture was picture perfect. St. Catherine's had seen to that. She could outsit even the headmistress herself on a straight-backed chair. Besides, what did it matter? She wasn't so sure that she really wanted a husband. Charlotte had apparently never married and she appeared perfectly happy. Maybe she would be better off living a life of seclusion as her father had planned. Charlotte, however, was determined not to let that happen, although her true strategy was not apparent to Amy until sometime later.

Almost immediately they began a series of excursions to the exclusive Bond Street apparel shops and dressmakers. Amy expected to have to endure the jostling of crowds of shoppers but Charlotte, for some obscure reason, chose a closed carriage with all the curtains drawn against the stares of the frankly curious. When Amy questioned her about the reason for the secrecy Charlotte replied that Society would have its chance at her in good time. But why she chose to use the State carriage, with its blatant elegance that plainly invited curiosity, was more than Amy could comprehend.

The visits to the dress shops entailed individual showings in the elegantly appointed private rooms of the establishment's owner. Amy and Charlotte invariably gained entrance through a discreet side door while the duke's carriage waited in brazen splendor. Charlotte always made a great show of introducing Amy as Lady Amy Dorset, daughter of the late Earl of Concord, but at the same time she pledged the proprietor to keep her identity a secret.

Upon leaving the establishment of Madame Delange, a particularly garrulous woman with mustard-colored hair, Charlotte could scarcely contain her laughter. She was breathing so hard that she had to revive herself with several sniffs from the vinaigrette which she carried in her reticule. Amy was concerned for her but Charlotte brushed it aside.

"It's nothing, child. I was just wondering who would be the first to hear about the Duke of Haddonfield's lovely new ward. I'll wager it's the next woman to enter the shop, providing there is no one there at the moment."

Amy was aghast. "But you pledged her to secrecy."

"Of course. And both she and I knew that a pledge to keep news like this a secret is the best way to insure that the word is spread. Don't you understand, child? Pretty young girls are forever being introduced to Polite Society. That's not news. But when someone tries to avoid public notice, particularly someone with your attributes, that is sensational news!"

She clasped her hands together in what amounted to ecstasy. "Why Amy, dear, this will be a thousand times better than a coming out. By the time we are ready to present you to the public the beau monde will be panting for a glimpse of you."

Amy was decidedly uneasy at the thought of so much attention. "But surely Jason will not permit such a thing to happen?"

Charlotte laughed. "My beloved nephew won't have a prayer of stopping it once I have set things in motion."

33

To Amy's intense relief Charlotte made no attempt to start her on a grand social whirl but permitted her to relax and enjoy the freedom of the huge estate. Jason was nowhere to be seen and Amy felt no need to be on her guard. On the day following their visit to Madame Delange calling cards were left by Sir Clement Atwood and Lord Clive Crancourt, the Sixth Baron of Penford. They were informed by Albert acting under Charlotte's instructions that Lady Amy Dorset was presently indisposed.

During the next few days a veritable blizzard of calling cards descended upon Haddonfield Hall. All were politely acknowledged, while at the same time an audience with Amy was refused by one cleverly invented pretext or another.

Amy was completely puzzled. Her armoire bulged with gowns, shawls, bonnets, riding costumes, and slippers enough to clothe all the students at St. Catherine's. They were made of lovely imported satins, brocades, and laces in shades of peach, apricot, blue, and brown that went so well with her creamy skin and bronze hair. But would Charlotte permit her to wear anything but her gray-on-gray or a few colorless dark blue gowns that made her skin look muddy? No! It was too much to comprehend.

Polly, at ease with Amy after having served as her personal maid since her arrival four weeks ago, was quite outspoken against Lady Charlotte's strict adherence to Jason's orders.

"Lawd!" she exclaimed. "What I wouldn't give to dress you in this 'ere." She pulled a misty green muslin from the cupboard and stroked the green velvet trim. "With your hair and those brown eyes, Beau Brummell hisself 'ud be pantin' after you."

Amy blushed. "Hush, Polly. You'll have me believing you if you continue these silly compliments."

"Silly, me foot." She cocked a curious eyebrow. "An wot does 'is lordship think about you in your pretty togs?"

"He has never seen me wear them." Amy fidgeted uncomfortably. "For one thing he is away a great deal."

"Aye. But 'e's comin' 'ome today." She pulled out a peach-colored satin gown cut daringly low in the bodice and held it against her, smoothing the fabric suggestively over her hips. "Why don't you wear this tonight and give 'is lordship a surprise?"

Amy giggled at the mischief in the girl's eyes but shook her head. "The idea is tempting but he would probably send me back to school if he saw me in that dress."

Polly smote her forehead with the flat of her hand. "Lawd! If you wait for 'is say-so these foin goods will rot where they 'ang." She peered cautiously from lowered lids. "'Is lordship may be a

35

foin gentleman an' all that, but if I do say so, 'e's a mite stuffy . . . 'im an' 'is books an' ledgers."

Amy thought about what the girl had said. It *was* a shame to have all those lovely gowns and not be able to wear them. Although Charlotte was reluctant to introduce Amy to Society, it surely couldn't matter if she wore a new gown at home. It was, after all, the custom to dress for dinner, and tonight Jason would be dining with them. If he followed his usual pattern of behavior he would probably not even be aware of her presence at the long, formal dining table.

Her eyes sparkled with excitement. "All right. I'll do it! Do you know," she said as she pulled her cap from her head, "he has never even seen my hair?"

"Lawd!" Polly grinned in delight. "I'd love to see 'is face."

It took the two of them to fasten Amy into the tight-waisted gown but the effect was worth the effort. Polly brushed and combed the copper curls until they crackled with hidden fires. When Amy was ready she stood in front of the Empire mirror and studied herself from head to toe. The results were astonishing.

Polly's hand flew to her mouth. "Blimey, it's a true beauty you've been 'iding all this time. Take my word for it, my lady. You goin' to set this town on its 'ead!"

Amy felt as if a stranger gazed back from the

mirror. She not only looked different, she felt different. She felt alive and glowing with an inner anticipation, as if she were about to open a lovely and unexpected gift.

At that moment Lady Charlotte tapped at the door and swept in nearly bursting with excitement. "It has finally come, Amy, the perfect—" She stopped abruptly. "What have you done, child? You are going to ruin everything."

Amy seemed to shrink within herself. "I—I'm sorry, Lady Charlotte. I only wanted to dress for dinner. Jason has yet to see any of my gowns." Her voice was small and childlike, reflecting the way she felt at having been reprimanded.

Charlotte's gaze took in Amy's appearance as she walked around the girl. Her smile was unspoken praise. "You'll do," she said, "except for the décolletage."

Polly ventured a remark. "Beggin' your pardon, mum, but 'tis high style now-a-days to show the bosom."

"All the more reason to cover it, gel. We'll add just a wisp of net to cover but not conceal it. I'll wager it will cause more than one dasher to want a closer look."

Amy blushed furiously. "Then I have your permission to wear it tonight?"

"Dear heaven, I almost forgot! No . . . no. Take it off and wear the dark blue. Be sure to cover your hair before you go downstairs." While

37

Polly grimly assisted Amy with the tiny buttons Charlotte thrust an expensively engraved invitation in front of her eyes. "This is what I have been waiting for. It's an invitation from the Prince Regent for Jason and his party to attend a grand fete at Carlton House in honor of the exiled Royal Family of France."

Polly drew an audible breath. "Gracious Lawd! From Prinny himself."

Charlotte bobbed her head. "The perfect place to introduce our girl to Polite Society."

Amy looked doubtful. "Do you think Jason will permit me to go?"

"Certainly not if you ask him like that! One must learn to use finesse. Leave it to me, Amy. You just make sure to come down to dinner in the dark blue . . . and wear your mobcap." She scurried to the armoire, shoving dresses aside as she rejected each one in turn. "We'll have to have a proper gown made for the occasion. Something dreadfully expensive and outstanding."

Charlotte's confidence encouraged Amy to a considerable degree but her own self-assurance began to slip some when they joined Jason in the study before dinner. He bowed distractedly to Amy in response to her curtsy, then turned to Charlotte as he shuffled through a stack of calling cards.

"Just what is all this, Aunt Charlotte? Are these

38

return calls? Have you been visiting all these people?" He looked dreadfully annoyed.

"Not at all, Jason. Amy and I have yet to make our first venture into Society. These are merely the cards of those who would like an opportunity to meet Lady Amy. I can't imagine how they could have heard . . . unless you . . ."

He blushed. "I may have mentioned that my father had been appointed guardian of a schoolgirl, but that should hardly have caught the interest of"—he flipped the cards—"Lord Trevor Hanshire, the Baron de Waxthorne, Sir Garson Flynn. There are dozens of them."

"Yes, so I have noticed. It is becoming apparent, your lordship, that I am remiss in my duties. It is time to choose an appropriate occasion for Amy to put in an appearance, lest we insult someone of political importance."

Jason stroked his chin. "Yes, I'm sure you are right. Confound! It's a tedious responsibility."

Amy hardly dared breathe. Standing silently while the two of them discussed her, she felt like an invisible intruder. She wanted to run up to Jason and tell him that she could take care of herself. She detested being beholden to him and it was clear from his attitude that he was less than happy with the added burden. A quick glance from Charlotte warned her to be silent.

Charlotte poured a glass of sherry and handed it to Jason who accepted it as she spoke. "I see

39

the messenger left an invitation to a reception for the Bourbon family at Carlton House."

"Umm . . . but if truth be told the Regent is giving the reception in honor of himself and his appointment to the Regency."

"You are going, of course?"

"Out of necessity. It would be politically unwise to absent myself, though it is difficult to imagine that the Prince would miss me. It is said the guests will number over two thousand."

Charlotte's voice barely betrayed her excitement. "It would be the perfect time to present Amy, don't you think? Your presence would add a fine sense of dignity and decorum."

Jason sipped his wine slowly. "I am planning to escort Lady Warrington."

Amy felt a sickening lurch somewhere in the pit of her stomach. Her face turned a degree whiter as she looked at Charlotte who set her glass down and smiled brightly.

"Of course, Jason. It is only right that you take Lady Elizabeth. After all, it would be expected. I rather think that we shall permit Count Borelli to escort us. He has been most persistent . . . left his card three times, if I recall."

Jason spluttered into his glass. "Egad! Charlotte, you can't be serious. The man is a bounder, a rake. No self-respecting girl would be seen with him."

"But he comes from a fine family, Jason, and

40

Amy would certainly not be alone with him. I am an accomplished chaperon."

He laced his fingers behind his back and paced the room. "Nevertheless I think it might be wise if I escorted my charge. As you say, it would add a significant touch of decorum."

"And Lady Elizabeth Warrington?"

"Can attend with her father."

"Well, whatever you say, Jason." She sighed. "It's settled then. As always, you know best."

He bowed in acknowledgment. Charlotte, her back to Jason, winked at Amy.

"I hope you are not too disappointed, child."

Amy shook her head. Amazed would be the word. Charlotte had guided Jason to his decision as surely as if he had a bit in his mouth and she held the reins. He not only cantered to her demands but pulled the cart as well. She couldn't help feeling sorry for him. Despite his serious nature there was something about him which appealed to her.

The thought of riding with him in the carriage and possibly sitting next to him at the long banquet table sent an unexplainable warmth rushing through her veins. Maybe for once he would see her for what she was: a living, breathing woman and not just a silly schoolgirl or an unavoidable obligation.

CHAPTER THREE

Amy and Charlotte spent the next few days shopping for material for the gown Amy was to wear to the Carlton House reception. Although white was considered most suitable for a young lady making her entrance into Society, Charlotte insisted that it would simply not do for Amy with her copper hair and pale skin. She rejected bolts of peach lace, yellow muslin, blue brocade, and a veritable rainbow of satins. Finally, in a tiny shop just off Hanover Square, she found a bolt of Japanese silk in a rich ivory, the color of Devonshire cream. The material was etched with darker ivory thread in a scrolled pattern that gave the fabric a look of pure elegance. Charlotte snapped it up at once and held it against Amy's skin as she pulled a curl from under Amy's bonnet.

42

"I knew we would find just the thing if we persisted long enough," she chuckled in triumph. "You can wear the sapphire silk cape and the matching slippers. Do you like the combination, Amy?"

Amy ran her fingers over the rich, heavy bodied silk. "I think it would be exquisite. It's the most beautiful piece of fabric I have ever seen." A frown creased her forehead. "But I wonder, can I really afford to spend so much? I have already spent a great deal on new gowns and slippers."

"Consider it an investment. This little gown would charm the Prince Regent himself if you wanted him."

Amy giggled. "Oh, Aunt Charlotte, stop teasing me. Polly said that he's terribly fat, not to mention the fact that he is forty-eight years old and already married to the Princess Caroline."

"She should have added the fact that he is over a hundred thousand pounds in debt. Not that it makes any difference. I doubt that they will carry the Regent off to debtor's prison."

"I wouldn't want to marry just for money. I've lived all my life without closets full of gowns and I never really felt deprived."

"Ah, yes, but that was before you had a taste of the finer things life has to offer. In a few weeks when you have been wined and courted by the nobility, you will tell a different tale."

They were still discussing the subject as they

rode home in the carriage. Amy brushed a bit of dust from her white glove. "I was just thinking of Jason. He has a great deal of money but it seems to afford him little pleasure. He is always so concerned about the management of the estate that he never has time to laugh."

Charlotte nodded in agreement. "It's true. He does take life very seriously. He did, even as a child. When he rode around the estate on horseback with his father, the servants used to call him 'the little gentleman' because he sat so straight and looked so serious."

"But surely he must find some pleasure in life. I—I overheard him say something about Lady Elizabeth Warrington," Amy said cautiously. "I—is she a particular friend of his?"

Charlotte laughed. "Particular? Yes, but as to the way you intended it, I really couldn't say. Her family owns the Candleworth Estate and it has always been taken for granted that she and Jason would one day marry. Of course I am in no position to question him about his intentions and he has never confided in me. I am fairly certain that he sees her frequently both here and at Almack's . . . and of course at private functions. But I have no idea how serious he is." Charlotte looked at Amy with curiosity, causing Amy to flush. "What makes you ask, Amy?"

"I—I think perhaps I am feeling guilty that Jason will be required to escort me to the fete when he would prefer to take Lady Elizabeth." Charlotte seemed satisfied with the explanation and settled back to watch the passing scenery. Amy felt a pang of conscience. She really didn't feel guilty that Jason would be taking her, she only felt a heady excitement beginning to build as each day rolled by. She did, however, feel badly about deceiving Charlotte.

During the next few days a skilled dressmaker was commissioned to create a gown for Amy out of the Japanese silk. Charlotte and Madame Corrine struggled for hours over the design that they hoped to select from the latest issues of the *Ladies' Quarterly* or *La Belle Femme*. The madame was determined to embellish the material with hundreds of tiny pearls which she thought to sew onto the fabric with delicate invisible stitches. Charlotte argued that she didn't care to follow the latest trend. What she wanted was something different, something uniquely eye-catching.

She spread the silk over the back of a chair letting it trail onto the burgundy carpet. The ivory silk etched with darker ivory thread was definitely Greek in design. "That's it!" She clapped her hands in triumph. "What we want is a simple Grecian design. Perhaps a drape over one shoulder leaving the other shoulder bare." The seamstress made quick sketches on a yellow tablet. Charlotte practically wept. "Yes, yes. That's it. What do you think, Amy?"

Amy nodded. "I like it. It's very plain and simple; not something I would have to be fussing with all evening. Will it be proper, though . . . leaving my shoulder bare?"

"But of course. While the other young ladies are practically baring their entire bosoms, we will permit just a glimpse of your shoulder as the tiniest bit of enticement. Look," she held the material against her body. "See how it clings and yet conceals? What a refreshing change it will be from those wetted-down and plastered-on muslins!"

The work on the dress was begun the same day. It was completed the morning of June 19 and by seven o'clock that evening Amy was getting dressed for the fete. Jason had yet to see her becomingly dressed and with her hair uncovered. As the time drew closer she had worked herself into a state of nervous apprehension.

Polly was overjoyed at the picture Amy made standing in front of the full-length mirror. "Oh, my lady," she murmured. "This will be a come out that will make Carlton 'ouse sit up and stare." Her brown eyes snapped with excitement. "Mark wot I say, before the week is out you'll receive your bid from Almack's."

Charlotte tapped at the door and came in bearing a small sandalwood box. She stopped short as she saw Amy, then slowly walked around her like a sculptor admiring his work. "Umm, I was

46

right, wasn't I?" She opened the velvet lined box. "There is just one thing it needs." Taking a small diamond and sapphire clip from the box, she pinned it to the gathers below Amy's shoulder. "This was given to me many years ago by someone very dear to me. I want you to keep it until you are betrothed. At that time you will no doubt be given jewelry of your own and you may, if you like, return it."

The clasp was made for the gown but Amy hesitated. When she started to protest Charlotte shushed her. "It would please me if you wore it, Amy."

On impulse Amy reached over and kissed the woman on the cheek. To her surprise Charlotte dabbed at her eyes with the back of her hand, adjusted her rose of Sharon crepe skirt, and scurried to the door.

"Enough of this, Amy. We must not keep Jason waiting." As an afterthought she turned. "Before you go downstairs to meet Jason, I think it might be wise to put on your cape and fasten the hood over your hair." Amy looked puzzled but Charlotte fluttered her hand. "Just do as I say. I shall do the same with my own cape."

With Polly's assistance she did as she was told. And suddenly it was time to go downstairs. Polly wished her well and for a fleeting instant Amy would have given anything if it were Polly going in her place. She summoned all her courage and,

47

gathering her skirts, began to descend the stairway. She was grateful for the sturdy railing because her knees began to shake before she was halfway down. The footman and lackeys greeted her with obvious approval as she swept past them to join Charlotte and Jason in the small salon.

As she curtsied Jason paused in the act of taking a sip of wine, bowed, and carefully set the glass on the silver tray. Never taking his gaze away from her, he came toward her. Amy was vaguely aware of Charlotte in the background. Summoning what courage she had she beamed a smile at Jason. "Good evening, your lordship. I hope I haven't detained you."

He didn't respond but stood in front of her, hands on hips, feet spread wide apart. Then he turned to Charlotte. "The cape is lovely but isn't it a trifle dramatic for one so young? I was under the impression that debutantes were expected to wear white."

Charlotte's tone was guarded. "One would hardly call this a proper debut, Jason. It was your wish, as I recall, that Amy make an informal debut into Society." She adjusted the embroidered cape over her rose crepe. "White is not becoming to Amy."

His voice had a cutting edge as he turned to Amy. "Pray tell, just what color *is* your gown?"

She hardly spoke above a whisper. "The gown is ivory, my lord."

48

He looked relieved. "Perhaps you would care to show it to me?"

Behind him Charlotte spread her hands in resignation and nodded to Amy, who began to remove the cape as Jason stepped closer to assist her. Laying it over the back of a chair he stood back and looked at her. Amy tried to read his thoughts but it was only when she saw the grim set of his mouth that she realized the extent of his displeasure. He turned to Charlotte with undisguised anger.

"Really, Charlotte, you must have lost your senses if you imagine that I shall permit her to attend the gala looking like this."

Amy's nerves had reached the breaking point. Before Charlotte could answer, Amy drew herself up to full height and knotted her fingers to keep them from shaking. Her voice sounded tinny to her ears as she faced Jason.

"Must you always converse as if I am not here? I am perfectly capable of understanding the spoken word. There is no need to address me through an intermediary. It is I who am to blame if my appearance displeases you, your lordship."

He clasped his hands behind his back. "In that event, Lady Amy, would you be so kind as to return to your chambers and exchange this . . . this gown for something more appropriate?"

Tears threatened to spill down Amy's cheeks and

her chin began to wobble, but she forced herself to stand her ground. "No, your lordship. I will not do that. If the truth be known it is me of whom you disapprove, not the dress." She saw him through a mist of tears. He looked as if he had been slapped and it gave her courage to go on. "Why did you bring me here if you dislike me so? Wh—why didn't you let me stay at school?"

He stared at her in disbelief, but before he could say anything, Amy whirled around and ran from the room. Polly was tidying up the bedchamber when Amy burst through the doorway and threw herself on the bed. The abigail gave a small cry of dismay.

" 'Ello, wot's goin' on 'ere?"

Amy buried her face in the pillow. "Please go away, Polly. I want to be alone." She could no longer control the rush of emotion which threatened to overwhelm her. For the first time in five years she cried as if her dreams had collapsed around her. At the same time she felt like a person divided into two parts. The other part of her seemed to watch the display of tears with a profound lack of understanding. The party at Carlton House really didn't mean so much to her that staying home should reduce her to tears. If truth be told she rather dreaded making her appearance at such a gathering. Why, then, the tears?

Seeing in her mind's eye the look of disappointment on Jason's face brought another flood of tears. *He* was the reason for her unhappiness. She had wanted so much to please him on this special night. She had worked so hard for his approval. Instead he had sent her to her room like a child in disgrace. As she sniffed Amy felt someone bump the bed. Opening her eyes she saw Jason, through a veil of tears, standing beside the four-poster, his hand outstretched.

"Here, Amy. I thought you could use a handkerchief."

He looked considerably less grim as she reached for the square of white linen. Indeed there was a hint of softness in his blue eyes that seemed to regard her with genuine concern.

Amy tried to hide her embarrassment by attempting to rise, but it was awkward, the bed being so high. He reached down to help her then stood facing her, his hands on her arms. As she looked up at him the vein at the side of his temple began to throb and his voice caught.

"I—I think perhaps we need to have an understanding." She nodded, too upset to know what to say as he continued. "There are a number of things I should have said to you before now."

Unaccountably Amy felt herself begin to sway toward him. His hands were still on her arms and he dropped them suddenly and swore under his breath. "I think it would be more proper if we were to retire to your sitting room. Charlotte would have my skin if she saw us here."

Amy blew her nose as she preceded him to the adjoining room. It took a concentrated effort to make her feet respond. The thought that hammered in her brain was: *He's going to send me away,* and it nearly broke her heart.

Jason seated her in a chair, then moved a few feet away to lean an elbow against the mantelpiece. As he stood there in contemplation Amy noticed how handsome he was in his tight-fitting, dove-gray breeches and matching coat. A pleated silk shirt and neckcloth edged in red and black piping was in the same soft shade of gray. She wanted to remember him as he was now . . . if she had to go back to school. For several minutes he stared at the toes of his black-top boots and when he spoke it was with obvious effort.

"I . . . ah . . . am not used to having to make an apology. For the most I am quite skilled at what I do. But unfortunately I have never learned to be a father."

Amy looked up in surprise. Father! Never for one moment had she thought of him as her father. Was this the manner in which he perceived their relationship?

He continued. "Charlotte tells me I have committed a grave injustice and I am inclined to agree with her. To begin . . . I most assuredly wish to advise you that . . . "—he shifted uncomfortably—"that you are here because I wish you to be. Furthermore" —he cleared his throat—

52

"my reaction tonight was in no way meant to indicate that I did not like the way you looked. In truth I was most unsettled to discover that you are a very beautiful girl."

He stole a glance at her, but meeting her gaze, Jason looked quickly away. His voice regained a measure of its old assurance. "The reason for my displeasure was the sure and certain knowledge that once we have introduced you into Society, there will be no possible means by which we can abide by your father's wishes. I saw that tonight and it frightened me."

Amy rose quickly and went over to stand beside him. Her voice betrayed her eagerness to believe his words. "Are you trying to tell me, your lordship, that you are not entirely disappointed in me?"

A smile lifted the corners of his mouth. "Could one be disappointed in a blossoming rose?"

Amy felt her heart sing. "Then I may stay here in this beautiful house . . . with you?"

"For as long as you wish. Lady Charlotte and the servants would feel cheated if they were deprived of your company."

Amy noted that he had neglected to include himself. She folded her hands gravely. "I shall try not to be a burden, your lordship. It is to my shame that I have been the cause of your missing the Prince Regent's gala."

"The fete will continue into the morning, Amy.

53

We can still arrive in ample time for the festivities. I'll call your abigail to help you fix your hair."

"Perhaps you should go without me. Lady Warrington would doubtless be pleased to see you."

"Nonsense. We shall go together or not at all." He turned faintly pink. "It will not be necessary to change your gown."

Amy dimpled at his discomfort. On impulse she leaned close and brushed a kiss against his cheek. "Thank you, Lord Jason. I shall try to do you credit."

He walked awkwardly toward the door, seemingly unsure of how to make a dignified exit. At the last moment he bowed deeply. "As I recall I had asked you to address me as Jason."

Amy nodded, equally as grave, and curtsied.

It was good to settle back in the carriage after the flurry and rush of getting ready for a second time. Jason, apparently lost in thought, rode in silence. Amy, less nervous now that she knew Jason approved of her, was content to listen to Charlotte who was by far the most excited of the three. She leaned across to touch Jason's knee with her gloved fingers.

"Is it true that none of the ladies of the Royal Family plan to attend? I have heard that two of the Regent's mistresses, Mrs. Fitzherbert and Lady Hertford, have been invited."

54

Jason glanced at Amy in alarm. She smiled impishly. "It is perfectly all right, Jason. I am well aware of those things." Her face turned scarlet. "Well, not out of hand, you understand."

He smiled wryly. "That is certainly to be hoped. As to the question, it is my understanding that when Mrs. Fitzherbert heard that Lady Hertford, instead of she, would be seated at the royal banquet table, she declined the invitation. It is to be noted, my dear Charlotte, that Lady Hertford is merely the Regent's companion, not his mistress."

Charlotte clucked her tongue. "If you believe that, my lord, you must believe the Whigs are back in power."

They were nearing the end of Knightsbridge Road and were about to enter Pall Mall. St. James's Street and the Haymarket were jammed with gilded coaches and carriages which stood in line to wait for their noble owners. Their progress slowed to a crawl as they joined the queue waiting to discharge their passengers. Up ahead the music from the Band of Guards, which played under the beautiful Henry Holland Corinthian portico, mingled with the crack of coachmen's whips and the rasp of iron-rimmed wheels on cobblestone.

When at long last it was their turn the coachman with the aid of the groom managed to quiet the skitterish horses, while the footman handed the passengers down to the carpeted runway. They were met by the Regent's servants in blue livery with gold lace, who ushered them into the great hall.

Jason handed his card and spoke to the head butler who bowed in recognition. Then, turning aside, the butler announced their names to the assembled guests in a powerful, stentorian voice.

At first Amy didn't realize what was happening. The magnificent architecture, the elegantly dressed people, and the profusion of gold and jewels wherever she looked had a tendency to dull the senses. She stood next to Jason with Charlotte just slightly behind them. As the impact of Jason's name spread across the room heads turned in their direction and conversation stopped in midsentence. The silence swelled across the assembly like a fast moving tidal wave.

Amy stood petrified. What had happened? The footman had taken her cape and she stole a look at her dress. No, everything was as it should be. She looked up at Jason who chuckled softly as he handed her his arm.

"I think Lady Charlotte has won the first skirmish." He sighed in resignation. "Lady Amy, shall we go through the receiving line?"

CHAPTER FOUR

There was no doubt in Amy's mind that they were all staring at her. Had it not been for Lady Charlotte's reassurance and Jason's firm hand on her arm, she would have panicked and run, but she managed somehow to get through the ordeal of the receiving line. Although no members of the Prince's immediate family were present, his brother, the Duke of Clarence, and another brother, Fredrick, the Duke of York, were among those who welcomed the guests in the great hall.

Amy breathed a prayer of gratitude for the rigorous training in polite etiquette she had undergone at St. Catherine's. She knew the proper time to curtsy and when to extend her hand to have it kissed. Upon seeing the admiring looks in the eyes of the gentlemen and the envy in the eyes of their ladies, Amy's confidence grew until she felt quite comfortable in the extravagant setting. At the same time she admitted to feeling like a princess in a fairy tale that would end when she awoke the next morning.

The Duke of Clarence informed Jason that the Regent had made his appearance promptly at nine fifteen to introduce his guests, the various members of the Bourbon family of French royalty. He also added that he was sure the Prince Regent would be devastated if he missed the opportunity to personally greet Lady Amy and welcome her to Carlton House.

Jason bowed in response to this but made no comment. After leaving the receiving line, Jason asked the ladies if they would care to browse through the social rooms to view the famous Carlton House collection of paintings and other objects of art. Both Charlotte and Amy said they would enjoy it but it was some time before they could escape the crush of people who wished to be presented to Amy. Then, shortly after 2:00 A.M., Jason was advised that the Prince was about to dine. Since Jason and his party were among the two hundred people selected to sit at the royal table, they were escorted to the huge, gothic conservatory where long tables were set beneath the lofty fan-vaulted ceiling. Ornate lanterns suspended at close intervals illuminated the elaborate tables which were laid with fragile crystal and heavy silver flatware. Fragrant smoke arising from tall silver urns mingled with the scent of roses and expensive perfumes. At half past two the assembled guests rose as the Regent and his party seated themselves at the head table.

When Prince George had passed by her table Amy was repelled yet fascinated by his appearance. His well-cut pantaloons betrayed the fact that he was snugly corseted and his lacings did little to conceal the great rolls of flesh. Although Amy recognized the fact that at one time the Prince must have been quite handsome, the heavy pastes and oils with which he painted his face gave a sickly, waxlike pallor to his skin. She leaned close to Charlotte and whispered, "What is wrong with his whiskers? They look very strange."

Charlotte lifted her fan to her face. "Prinny likes to supplement his meager beard with false whiskers pasted to his cheeks." She chuckled. "And that isn't the only thing about him that is an artifice. Did you notice the field marshal's insignia on his uniform? George the Third would never consent to give him the rank so he gave it to himself. If the King weren't already mad that would have driven him to madness."

Jason shot her a warning look which effectively silenced her, then he leaned close so they both could hear. He nodded toward the Regent's table. "Seated on the Prince's right is the Duchess d'

Angoulême, the only living child of Louis XVI. On his left is the Duchess of York who is the wife of the Prince's eldest brother."

Amy was too awed to do anything but stare. On the table in front of the Prince Regent was created a forest scene with a silver fountain spilling water into a miniature lake which divided into two silver-bedded streams. The streams were lined on each side with ferns and mosses from which delicate star-shaped flowers sprang in profusion. Gold and silver fish swam beneath arched bridges except for an occasional fish which floated dead upon the surface of the water. Amy saw one of the poor creatures gasping for breath and tears stung her eyes. She tried to brush them away without being seen but Jason's observant glance caught the motion.

His voice was dry. "Don't waste your tears on a senseless fish, child, when half of Britain is starving to pay for this fete."

It wasn't his rebuke which dried her tears, it was the word *child*. She hated condescension more than physical pain. With a determined lift to her chin she made up her mind to show Jason that others might not treat her so lightly. With her elbow on the table, chin resting on her hand, she leaned forward and flashed a brilliant smile at the young dandy seated across the table. He put his wineglass down so quickly that some of the contents stained the tablecloth. Half knocking over

60

the silver champagne bucket, he stood and executed an awkward bow, much to the irritation of the young woman seated next to him.

"Allow me to present myself, if I may be so bold. I am the third Earl of Colshire and this is my friend, Miss Margaret Elaine Belden."

Amy extended her hand, then presented Lady Charlotte and Jason, whom he had previously met. The young woman accepted the introductions sulkily but refused to join in the conversation that continued through the meal.

To Jason's obvious discomfort and Lady Charlotte's undisguised pleasure, a number of young men on either side of the table joined in the lively conversation with an exchange of impressions of the extravagant display. One debonair young dasher, a proclaimed follower of Beau Brummell who believed that elegance of dress was at its finest when it spoke softly, laughed aloud at the Regent's ornately embroidered coat.

Jason looked sternly at the young man. "You find our Prince to be an object of amusement?"

"Oh, rather!" He grinned. "It's said that the cost and the weight of his coat are the same . . . two hundred pounds."

The comment brought a roar of approval from the listeners and Jason, being forced to accept defeat, settled back with a dark look on his face. Before the first course was finished a half dozen young men had made it plain that they were interested in plying Amy with their favors. A great many heads had turned in their direction, first with expressions of curiosity at the commotion, and then with frank admiration at the attractive picture Amy made in her ivory gown.

The champagne glasses were never allowed to remain empty thanks to the attentive footmen, one of whom was positioned behind every fourth guest. Sixty footmen attended the Regent and his guests at the head table over which was suspended from a silver crown a velvet curtain embroidered with the initials G.R. One of the footmen wore a full suit of heavy armor. Amy felt real sympathy for the man inside. The ceiling fans helped to dispel some of the heat but Amy thought he must surely be nearly suffocating.

The dinner consisted of dozens of dishes, among which were glazed fowl, hot soups, roasts, tempting jellied salmon, cold meats, and pastries. Fresh fruits such as peaches, grapes, and fragrant imported pineapple were stacked high in silver compote bowls so everyone might eat their fill. The entire dinner service from soup plates to tureens to platters were cast of solid silver, not only in the main dining area but in the countless side rooms which were set up to serve less favored guests.

By the time magnificent trays of glacé fruit and nuts were brought out Amy had begun to feel nauseated at the very thought of food. Her stomach, which for so many years had been used to simple fare, began to rebel at the rich and spicy sauces. It was with gratitude she saw the Regent rise and escort his party to the side rooms where they would mingle with the less important guests.

Lady Charlotte tipped her fan and leaned toward Jason. "Is it your plan to present Amy to the Regent before the night is past?"

He scowled. "Not without a royal command. Indeed, I think it prudent that we leave as early as is proper."

Charlotte looked amused. "Surely, my lord, you are not apprehensive where the Prince is concerned? I'm told he prefers older women."

"I know you speak in jest, Charlotte, but the Prince has an undeniable gift of charm despite his obesity. I have no intention of tempting fate on that score."

As the guests removed themselves from the table the most curious gravitated to the massive gilt pillars where Jason stood with his party in preparation to leave. A handsome young officer in the uniform of the Prince's own regiment, the 10th Light Dragoons, a trifle bolder than the others, braved Jason's scowl.

"With your lordship's permission, sir, I would request the privilege of showing her ladyship some of the Regent's art treasures which are on display in the small drawingroom."

Jason's voice was a growl. "I appreciate your thoughtfulness, Captain Kinsgrove, but I rather

63

think Lady Amy wishes to leave. It has been a tiring day and she is unused to keeping late hours."

Amy tried to keep the irritation from her voice. She *was* tired and she would have liked to go to bed, but not at the cost of being treated like a little girl. She put her hand on Jason's arm.

"I'm perfectly wide awake, my lord," she said in a honeyed voice, "and I wouldn't dream of taking you away from this splendid gala. I'm sure Lady Charlotte and I would be delighted to have Captain Kinsgrove escort us to the exhibit."

Jason's face reddened above the high starcher and he bowed stiffly. "Very well, Lady Amy. If that is your wish I shall join you within the hour in the main foyer." He turned abruptly and strode away.

Charlotte winked but Amy felt no triumph as she took the captain's arm without giving the young officer a second glance. He seemed so unimportant somehow.

With Jason safely out of the way the crowd of young bucks took courage to present themselves. Amy was particularly entertained by the Marquis of Melmoth, a tall, distinguished gentleman with straight black hair which had begun to gray at the temples. He shared her interest in a group of delicate porcelain figurines which were displayed in a glass case recessed into the wall.

In the small drawingroom which would have contained five rooms the size of the dormitory at

St. Catherine's, Amy was amazed by the outrageous collection of art the Regent had amassed. Lady Sarah Spencer, who proved to be a dear friend of Lady Charlotte, shook her head in disbelief.

"My husband and I have been to Carlton House many times but I am always surprised at what I see," she said in aside to Amy. "My husband is a close friend of the Duke of Clarence, the Regent's brother. His Highness changes the exhibits so frequently that I have yet to view the same painting twice."

Lady Charlotte spoke up. "I was hoping to see some of Mr. Constable's work. They say he is an upcoming artist."

"Yes," the woman agreed. "Unfortunately he hasn't enough connections to get anywhere at the Royal Academy, at least if Benjamin West has anything to say about it."

They wandered across the room leaving Amy surrounded by her would-be suitors. One baby-faced boy was practically begging for attention.

"May I fetch you a glass of champagne, Lady Dorset, or anything else?" he finished weakly.

"Thank you, no. I have had a sufficiency of both food and champagne. I confess I am not used to such extravagance." She smiled, hoping to put him at ease. "But you are very kind to offer." He blushed to the roots of his fair hair.

Captain Kinsgrove had tried by every possible ploy to get Amy to himself but without success.

She was flattered by the attention but at the same time thought that most of the young men seemed silly and affected. Their conversations consisted mainly of extravagant compliments, remarks about the Prince's overdisplay of wealth, and wagers on the latest bout of fisticuffs. She agreed that Carlton House was oppressively ornate. Someone said that the decor was only slightly less sumptuous than the Versailles Palace. Amy found the excessive use of gold and silver ornamentation to be more ostentatious than beautiful.

When Amy expressed admiration for a tall basket of carnations Captain Kinsgrove plucked one and placed it in her hair just above her ear. "A study in contrast, your ladyship. Your beauty makes the flower seem ugly in comparison."

Amy turned pink at the ridiculous compliment. "Really, Captain Kinsgrove. I may be inexperienced but I hope you don't expect me to allow such remarks."

He bowed with a flourish that displayed his well-cut uniform most effectively. "Your inexperience only adds to your charm, my lady. It has been a long time since the beau monde has seen anyone with your freshness and appeal. Am I not right, gentlemen?"

"Hear, hear!" They lifted imaginary glasses in a toast.

"Tell us," he continued, "now that you have left the academy behind you and are living at

Haddonfield Hall, what do you plan to do with Concord Hou. . . ?"

Before he could finish the sentence Lady Charlotte cut into the conversation with uncustomary rudeness. "I really think it is time we joined his lordship in the foyer, Lady Amy." Her tone left no room for argument. Amy, seeing her chaperon's mouth set in a firm line, lifted her skirt and turned to follow her with a hasty expression of apology to her admirers.

Tired as she was, Amy nearly floated downstairs. For the first time in her life she had been accepted as a woman and knew full well that she could pick and choose among the dozen or so men who had courted her attention. Oddly enough none of them truly appealed to her, with the possible exception of the Marquis of Melmoth, Lord Andrew Graham. She admitted an eagerness to get to know the man better.

Lady Charlotte, totally aware of the heads which turned their way as they passed through the orderly gathering, was practically glowing with pleasure. "Amy, my dear, it might well be that you have become the latest rage among the ton. Your head will surely be turned if I confide all the things people are saying about you." She squeezed Amy's hand. "Isn't it just too exciting?"

Amy smiled, knowing full well that it was Charlotte who most enjoyed the coup. "I have never experienced anything so exciting in all my life, Lady Charlotte, and I owe it all to you."

"Hardly. Though if truth be told I'm absolutely thrilled to be a part of it." She paused. "Oh, my. I would really like to take the time to study this tapestry. It is the one treasure that isn't gilded . . . but we really mustn't keep Jason waiting."

If decorum would have permitted, Amy would have run to keep up with her eagerness to find Jason. For the life of her she did not understand why. At best, he was critical of her. Why, when there were so many men eager to fall at her feet, should she want to be with him who sought only to lecture her? They had been gone over an hour and he was sure to be discomfited.

But Jason was not waiting alone in the grand entrance hall. Amy knew without having to ask that the cool, elegant pink-and-blond beauty who clung to his arm was Lady Elizabeth Warrington. Grudgingly Amy admitted that in addition to her natural loveliness, the woman was dressed with exquisite taste. Her gown was a pale lilac muslin chemise, gathered with a narrow ribbon just below the bustline. The rounded neckline, cut enticingly low, was edged with tiny artificial flowers which were repeated in a wide band at the hem. A filmy cape effect of the same lilac muslin floated back from the shoulders to end in a demitrain almost at the floor. But it was her hair that added the regal touch. She wore it in a high coronet interspersed with strands of flowers and pearls. At the back a cluster of ringlets gleamed like clover honey in the glow of the lanterns.

As the woman glanced up and saw them approach she stepped even closer to Jason, whispering something that caused him to smile. He said something in return and patted the slender hand where it lay on his arm. Amy gritted her teeth and straightened her shoulders, fighting the constriction in her throat. Jason turned then and spoke to the distinguished-looking white-haired gentleman who stood nearby. *Lady Warrington's father,* Amy thought. *Jason said he would act as her escort.*

This proved to be true a few minutes later when Jason made the presentations. Amy prayed that she looked less dismal than she felt as she curtsied to acknowledge the introductions. The earl was as gallant and courtly as he appeared to be, but Lady Elizabeth, although it could have been Amy's imagination, seemed cool and remote. Her voice, while not actually brittle, had a definite edge to it.

"How nice to finally meet you, Lady Amy. Jason has said so little about you that we were beginning to wonder if you really do exist."

The earl beamed at them. "Well, my dear, we can set our fears at rest. She is most certainly real. But I must confess to being surprised." His eyes twinkled beneath white eyebrows. "I fully expected to see a gauche and gangly schoolgirl instead of this charming and lovely young woman."

His words left a dead silence. Jason appeared flushed and uncomfortable, Lady Charlotte, smug and self-satisfied, and Lady Elizabeth, white-lipped and grim, looked to be in the first stage of a temper tantrum. For her own part Amy was somewhat embarrassed but she did manage a simple thank-you. Lady Charlotte finally saved the moment by making an inane comment about the masses of people, and a thread of conversation began again. A short time later a lackey interrupted to inform Jason that his carriage was waiting at the entrance. With the possible exception of the earl, everyone breathed a sigh of relief at the timely reprieve.

During the ride home Jason and Amy were silent, save for monosyllabic replies to Charlotte's chatter which in truth left no room for reply. The team of four sleek black horses, themselves no doubt anxious to be home after the long night, needed no crack of the whip to urge them on at a steady pace. The gentle rocking of the high-sprung carriage would normally have been enough to have set Amy to dozing but she was too restless to sleep. Jason, too, appeared nervous. Where other men might have resorted to a pipe or a pinch of snuff, Jason slapped his gloves rhythmically against the palm of his left hand.

Amy found the noise irritating and wondered what gave him such cause for peevishness. But of course! He was angry at having to leave Lady Elizabeth. He would have been free to enjoy the entire evening had it not been for his responsibility to supervise Amy. The thought only made her sink more deeply into a state of gloom.

Haddonfield Hall was dark save for a single light in the window of the entrance hall and the great torches beside the front door. Albert met them at the carriage as the driver and footman helped them down. The drowsy groom, wakened from a snooze on the jump seat, was still half asleep as he held the bridle of the lead team of blacks. Albert, impeccably dressed as always, ushered them up the short flight of steps.

"Cook has set a tray of pastries in the library, your lordship, and the chocolate will be ready in a moment, if it pleases you."

Jason raised an inquiring eyebrow. Charlotte nodded.

"Yes, that would be divine. I shall need something to relax me before I retire. I think it might be good for you, too, Amy." Albert went to tell the cook while they continued into the library. Lady Charlotte, looking as full of vigor as she had at the outset of the evening, paced the room in strides which seemed surprisingly long for her size. Jason slumped into a chair behind the desk while Amy seated herself primly upon the love

71

seat. Lady Charlotte smiled as she wrapped her arms around herself.

"Amy, my dear, this is a night for you to remember."

Jason looked up at her with a hint of sarcasm on his face. "I hope it worked according to plan, Aunt Charlotte. Did you achieve what you set out to do?"

She looked smug. "We made a fine beginning, my lord. Our girl has a bid for a drive in the park this afternoon. She also has an invitation to a party at Penridge Castle and has promised an 'at home' to any number of young dashers. You cannot deny that she was a great sensation."

Jason shook his head. "No, I'll not deny that point. I only wonder what her father would think."

"He would think that Amy has a fine opportunity to select an eligible young man of her own choosing . . . with your approval, of course," she amended hastily.

"And your inevitable maneuvering."

"I prefer to call it guidance."

It was a game between them and they both enjoyed it to the fullest, Amy observed. The two of them were like friendly combatants with their parry and thrust, and each admired the other for the subtle twist of the blade. Like it or not, she was the helpless pawn who stood between them.

Albert's arrival with the tray of chocolate put an end to the skirmish. Charlotte ate with considerable gusto and then, covering a yawn, excused herself for the night. Left alone with Jason, Amy was at a loss for words. When the silence grew oppressive she ventured a question.

"Have you often been a guest at Carlton House, Jason?"

He grunted. "More times than I care to count. As you may have perceived, I am not overly tolerant of the Regent's way of life. His Majesty, King George the Third, would have been appalled at tonight's needless display of wealth. If the Regent finally comes to full power, I'll wager he will squander away the kingdom with his high living."

"Then he has not yet achieved full power?"

"No, not for another year. This stipulation was added with the hope that the King might yet recover from his malaise in time to resume leadership."

"Is that likely to happen?"

He shook his head regretfully. "There is little hope in that direction. One hears many rumors, but the truth is that the King has passed well into the realm of madness. God only knows what will happen to the country now."

"It is my understanding that the Regent finds it most difficult to make decisions. Do you think he will bring the Whigs to power?"

Jason's laugh was sharp. "That is the question to which we all seek an answer, Amy."

"But it will logically happen, don't you think? I mean after all, history repeats itself. Young men always rebel against their fathers and princes against their kings. If for no other reason, the Regent will bring the Whigs to power to show that he is his own man and no longer under the thumb of his father."

Jason looked at her quizzically. "You seem well informed, Amy. It surprises me that one so young, particularly a girl, should find the subject of politics so fascinating." He got up and came around to perch on the edge of the desk. As he unconsciously swung his leg the soft cloth of his formal breeches clung tightly to his calves, outlining in full detail the fine ridge of muscle and bone just below the knee.

Amy looked quickly away. "It isn't just politics which interests me, Jason, it's people. I like to try to understand what makes them do the things they do."

He smiled. "You are truly an awakening to me. I have never been around a woman of your age, not to mention trying to understand why they do what they do. Now, with my chance at being a substitute father, perhaps I shall gain some insight into the matter."

He smiled and leaned close to pluck the carnation from her curls. "You have the most radiant hair I have ever seen. I hope, in the future, you will see fit to leave it uncovered while in the house. It is a joy simply to look at it."

"If that is your wish, Jason."

He stood so close that she could see the green flecks in his blue eyes. Beads of perspiration dotted his forehead. It was June 20, 1811. The weather was not at all warm, but strangely enough, Amy felt her temperature rising.

CHAPTER FIVE

Jason twirled the carnation between his fingers as a smile tugged at the corners of his mouth. "I see you have stolen a flower from the Regent's vase. Do you then share my appreciation for natural things?"

Amy nodded. "There is nothing more beautiful than a flower, but I did not steal it. Captain Kinsgrove placed it in my hair."

Jason swore softly and turned away. "It seems we are about to be plagued with hordes of panting young bucks." He crumpled the flower in his fist and threw it into the cold fireplace. Striding across the room, he turned as he reached the doorway. "Dawn will be here soon. I think it is best if you retire. I bid you good-night, Lady Amy."

He bowed and was gone before she could even speak.

Amy suddenly felt exhausted. She pondered Jason's abrupt change of mood as she all but dragged herself up the stairs after dismissing Albert and thanking him for his service. For a moment tonight she had seen almost tenderness in Jason's attitude. Why he chose so rarely to show this facet of his character Amy could not begin to guess, but she longed to know more about this fascinating man.

When Amy entered her bedchamber she found Polly fast asleep on the settee, no doubt waiting to assist Amy out of her gown. She looked so comfortable that Amy was careful not to waken her. But if truth be told, Amy preferred not to have to face a barrage of questions about the fete. She knew that Polly's curiosity would be running full tilt. Slipping out of her gown, she splashed cold water on her face and prepared for bed.

Promptly at four that afternoon Captain Harry Kinsgrove called at Haddonfield Hall in an open carriage. The elegant low-slung park phaeton, lacquered white with gold embellishments, was especially designed to show off its occupants while they took the afternoon air.

Amy, grateful to discard her drab clothing once and for all, selected a fetching gown of peach-colored muslin with a matching shawl which fas-

77

tened just below the bodice. The slightly flared skirt came just to the toe of her white kid slippers. Charlotte wore a sprigged muslin topped off with a white lace fichu and a ruby brooch. Captain Kinsgrove, looking very handsome and very young in his regimental uniform, beamed with pride as he handed the ladies into the carriage.

He bowed low. "I didn't think it possible but your ladyships are even lovelier in the light of day. I consider it an honor and pleasure to be your escort. Do you have a preference between Green or Hyde Park?"

Amy fastened the ribbons of her straw bonnet beneath her chin. "London is so new to me that I'm sure to be delighted with whichever you choose, Captain Kinsgrove."

"And you, Lady Winford?"

She waved a white-gloved hand. "I shall leave the choice to you young people."

He took the reins from the tousle-haired boy who served as groom. As soon as the youngster was seated on the jump seat at the rear, the captain gave the horses their head. It was a spirited team of matched bays and soon the horses were moving at a good pace down Upper Brook Street to the turn at Tiburn Lane. The captain sat back against the cushions, holding the reins loosely, as he pointed out the various places of interest along the way. He was careful to include Lady Charlotte

78

in the conversation, despite the fact that she was seated behind them.

He was an accomplished storyteller with a collection of funny anecdotes which, because of his youth, had to be either borrowed or fabricated, but this detracted not at all from the telling. Once they entered the gate to Hyde Park he slowed the horses to a walk. Elm trees arching over the drive provided enough shade that Amy and Lady Charlotte were able to lower their lace sunshades. For her own part Amy would have enjoyed the sun on her face, but Lady Charlotte declared it grossly unfashionable to allow the sun to color one's skin. Indeed the ladies of the ton who strolled with their gentlemen escorts in skin-tight trousers and high starched neckcloths, carried dainty parasols of lace or ruffled muslin to match their gowns.

As they rounded a bend in the Serpentine a smart looking vis-à-vis, driven by a servant in sparkling livery, slowed and drew alongside.

The captain doffed his silk top hat. "Good afternoon, Lady Cowper. What a pleasure to see you again."

The woman smiled warmly. "The pleasure is mine, my dear Captain Kinsgove." She laid a gloved hand on the ornate molding of the carriage as she leaned forward. "And you, Lady Charlotte. You look magnificent as always. We have seen much too little of you."

Charlotte fluttered her fan. "I fear that my

nephew has had little time to spend with the beau monde, Lady Cowper. Our loss, I'm sure. But it is to be hoped that the estate matters can take care of themselves, allowing us more free time now that Lady Amy is with us."

"Yes, my dear," the woman cooed. "I have heard about the duke's young ward but have yet to enjoy the pleasure of meeting her."

Charlotte feigned shock. "Please do forgive me. I was so sure that she had been presented to you." She made the introductions with a flourish. After the small carriage pulled away Lady Charlotte sat back with a smug expression on her face. "That, my dear, is one of the three absolute rulers of Almack's, the epitome of social clubs. Without her approval a girl has no chance at all to succeed in Polite Society."

The captain chuckled. "No offense, your ladyship. I would wager that Lady Amy Dorset would succeed without help from Almack's or the beau monde. With her beauty and expectations she will soon be the rage."

Amy turned pink. "Really, Captain Kinsgrove, you embarrass me. As for my expectations—"

Lady Charlotte cut in quickly. "I perceive the subject to be comparatively unimportant at this time."

It was the captain's turn to redden. "Oh, rawther, your ladyship. I only meant to offer a compliment."

80

"And so it was taken." Charlotte smiled. "I wonder, Captain, would you perhaps care to stroll for a while?"

He appeared relieved. "If it would please the ladies." He pulled the team to a halt, gave over the reins to the groom, and handed the ladies down.

At the fashionable hour of five o'clock Hyde Park was crowded with promenaders of the upper echelon of London Society. A great many expensively dressed couples paused to speak to Lady Charlotte with the transparent intention of being introduced to Amy. Several dowagers whom Charlotte knew to be the mothers of eligible sons casually let it be known that they would be receiving guests whenever Lady Charlotte and her charge cared to call. Lady Charlotte later pointed out that the sons were, for the most part, second sons who would stand to inherit little, save the bad habits passed on from generation to generation.

To Amy's pleasure she saw Lord Andrew Graham, the Marquis of Melmoth, appproaching somewhat shyly, yet with an eager expression on his face.

"Lady Amy, Your Grace," he bowed to the ladies, then briefly acknowledged Captain Kinsgrove. "I was hoping to see you in the park this afternoon while my daughters and I were taking the air. But perhaps you don't remember me.

81

There were so many admirers around you last night."

Amy smiled at the distinguished older man. "Of course I remember you, Lord Graham. As I recall we were both impressed by the Regent's collection of porcelain figurines."

The Marquis of Melmoth beamed his pleasure at having been remembered, as Amy continued. "Are those pretty little girls playing by the fountain really your daughters?"

He nodded. "Yes. The eldest is Anne, with the dark hair. The tall, pretty one is Margreth, and the one sitting so quietly is Sarah, my youngest." He answered the question in Amy's eyes. "Their mother died when Sarah was born."

"Oh, I'm so sorry. I'm sure the children, and you, of course, must miss her very much."

He nodded. "I wonder, my lady, if I might have the honor of calling upon you, with your guardian's permission, naturally?"

Amy felt unusually pleased. "Why yes, Lord Graham. I would like that very much."

He looked over at Captain Kinsgrove who was scowling most unpleasantly, and continued with a twinkle in his eyes. "There is a play at the Drury Lane Theatre that I'm told is exceptionally good. It would be my pleasure to escort you and Lady Winford tomorrow evening . . . or possibly you might prefer a concert?"

Amy had been about to say she preferred the

theatre when Lady Charlotte broke in with unusual rudeness. "I'm sure that Lord Jason will consent to the concert. I believe Haydn's *Salomon Symphonies* are to be performed at the Philharmonic Society this week."

His face brightened. "Excellent. I shall call for you at seven tomorrow evening, if that is acceptable." He bowed and excused himself, and none too soon judging from Captain Kinsgrove's sullen expression.

He drew himself up tall. "I wonder if we should perhaps return to the carriage?" he asked, forcing a smile. "The crowd is too large for a pleasant stroll." He regained his normally good humor once they were seated in the park phaeton.

They were tooling along at a fairly brisk pace, passing the slowest carriages but often being overtaken by the more adventurous drivers. Amy was amused to find that the captain had placed himself much closer to her the second time they got into the carriage. When his thigh grazed her hip for the barest fraction of a second, the touch was reflected by a slight trembling of his hands on the reins. She supposed she should have been feeling a tingling of her blood or a fluttering of her heart but all she could muster was a brief smile. He was older than Amy by several years but she was tempted to pat him on the top of his golden curls and say, "There, there, dear, it's all right."

He was talking about another of his small triumphs as an officer in the dragoons when the accident happened. One of the narrow iron-rimmed wheels had apparently become wedged in a rut between the cobblestones. As it turned it wrenched sideways, causing the carriage to lurch over until it was virtually on its side. Amy was thrown against Captain Kinsgrove who held onto her to keep her from being thrown to the ground, while at the same time keeping the horses from bolting. Lady Charlotte had let out a most unladylike yell when her elbow had grazed the wheel, but she appeared otherwise unhurt. The sturdy groom was thrown from the jump seat onto the roadway but was only slightly bruised. It had happened so quickly that no one had had time to be frightened.

As the crowd gathered around them Amy felt herself being lifted down to the ground. Settling her skirts primly over her ankles she looked up into the most handsome face she had ever seen. His cool gray-green eyes surveyed her with mischief as he continued to hold her. "Are you all right, my lady?" the gentleman inquired.

"Quite. But would you see to it that Lady Charlotte and the others are taken care of? I think she might be injured."

"They are presently being seen to. I believe their injuries are not serious."

Amy gently pulled free from his hold. "I thank

you for your kind assistance. My name is Lady Amy Dorset."

He bowed low with a graceful sweep of his silk top hat. "George Brummell at your service, your ladyship. May I offer you and your chaperon the use of my carriage? It appears that yours will require extensive repairs."

"That is very generous of you, sir, but I would hate to inconvenience you."

"It would be my pleasure."

"In that case let me speak to my escort and chaperon to see what arrangements are being made."

The captain was unhurt but a trifle muzzied by the accident that had damaged the carriage which had been rented from Tilbury's on Mount Street for the occasion. He agreed rather downheartedly to allow Beau Brummell to escort the ladies home. Only when Amy told him that she would be pleased to see him again did he take heart.

By comparison to the white-and-gold park phaeton, Beau Brummell's black cabriolet seemed sedate and yet far more elegant with the bewigged and powdered coachman sitting high above them in his three-cornered hat. Charlotte dusted her gown and settled back against the seat next to Amy.

"It was most kind of you, Mr. Brummell, to rescue us. I do hope we haven't taken you too far out of your way."

"Indeed not, Lady Winford. I was merely planning to attend the gaming tables at Watiers. In truth, you probably have rescued me. The way the cards have fallen lately I would no doubt have lost a good deal of money. So you see," he smiled disarmingly, "I am actually in your debt."

Amy had a chance to look closely at this man whose name she recognized as being the foremost authority on men's fashions. She had expected to see him wearing brilliant colors with an abundance of braid and embroidery. Instead, his clothing was extremely plain. It was the splendid cut and rich quality of the materials which spoke of elegance. She would have known without being told that here was a man who would lead rather than follow. She also knew that he would be equally at home with a king or a beggar in an alehouse. If his gaze left her a bit unsettled, his words jolted her.

"I trust you are enjoying your first ventures into London Society, Lady Amy? You are a most lovely addition to the beau monde." He looked closely. "You bear a very strong resemblance to your talented mother whom it was my great pleasure to see perform many times at Drury Lane and the Theatre Royal."

Charlotte sat bolt upright. "Yes. Well, it appears we are nearly home. Except for the fact that both Lady Amy and I are in need of repair, we would have been delighted to offer you refreshment, Mr. Brummell. Perhaps another time?"

86

"Indeed. It would be my pleasure."

Amy was mystified by Lady Charlotte's abrupt manner that bordered on rudeness. Mr. Brummell had been most kind. Moreover he was charming, extraordinarily handsome and witty, and Amy would have enjoyed spending more time with him. When he saw them to the door he bowed deeply to Lady Charlotte, then reached for Amy's hand and touched it to his lips. It seemed to Amy that he lingered overlong and the look in his eyes confirmed that it was deliberate.

"Good afternoon, ladies. I hope it will be my good fortune to have the pleasure of your company again soon."

Amy curtsied. "Thank you, Mr. Brummell. I only hope that the next time will be under more fortunate circumstances." She watched from the window as his carriage drove off down the street. Wonder of wonders! The king of the beau monde had kissed her hand . . . a thrill which most women dreamed of all their lives . . . and she had only experienced a mild amusement. She turned to follow Charlotte into the main entrance hall.

Albert was more than a little perturbed when he saw their dishevelled appearance and Amy's demolished sunshade. Charlotte explained briefly what had happened before they went upstairs to change. She accompanied Amy to her bedchamber and waited while Amy pulled the bell cord to summon her abigail.

"Amy, my dear, this accident today was a singular bit of good luck." Lady Charlotte's silvery curls danced as she strode across the room. "If I had planned it myself it couldn't have worked so nicely."

"I'm afaid I don't understand."

"Surely you couldn't have missed seeing those envious glances directed toward you while we were riding in Mr. Brummell's carriage? To be seen with Beau Brummell is a sure entrée into the most desired social sets in town."

Amy tried hard to match Lady Charlotte's enthusiasm, but at best, she could only pretend. When Polly arrived to help Amy change the entire incident had to be repeated detail by detail. To say that Polly was impressed would hardly do justice to the girl's reaction. She appeared to savor each morsel as if she were experiencing it herself. Indeed Amy felt a moment's regret that Polly could not have been there in her place. It would have meant so much more to the servant girl than it had meant to her.

Amy fingered the gowns in the armoire. "I believe I shall stroll in the garden before dinner, Polly. You may lay out the blue sprigged muslin. Jason seems to like blue."

"If it's 'is lordship you're aiming to please, miss,

88

you're wastin' your time. 'E told cook not to plan on 'im for dinner tonight."

"Oh, I see. On second thought I have changed my mind about the garden. I think I shall just rest for a while before dinner."

Polly helped her into a soft green dressing gown and began to brush her curls. When Amy cried out in pain Polly stopped abruptly.

" 'Ello, wot's this? You've gone and 'urt yourself, miss."

Amy looked into the hand mirror and saw a dark stain beginning to appear on her right temple. She fingered it gingerly. "It's nothing, just a bruise. I struck my head on the side of the carriage when the wheel gave way."

"Shall I put a cold compress on to draw out the pain?"

"No, thank you. It only pains when I touch it."

"A little rest might be the best medicine. I'll wake you in time to dress for dinner." She bound Amy's hair back with a gold velvet ribbon and turned the cover down on the bed.

With Polly out of the room Amy leaned back against the cool pillow and closed her eyes. The shine had gone out of the day when she learned that Jason would not be home for dinner. She felt a quick flush of guilt. It was selfish of her to want Jason to spend his evenings with her and she mentally chastised herself for being so thoughtless.

89

Still . . . she could not completely rid herself of the ache in the pit of her stomach at the thought of Jason having dinner with Lady Warrington. Was the woman his mistress? Amy couldn't accept that. Lady Warrington was too cool, too calculating to settle for a quick tumble. She would never lower her dignity to settle for anything less than marriage and the prospect of a title.

Amy turned pink. If truth be told she would never give herself to a man outside the sanctity of marriage either. Only a woman of limited virtue would consider such a thing. Surely this must be true? She fell asleep pondering the question.

It seemed like only a short time later that Polly was shaking her awake. "Do wake up, Lady Amy. You must hurry."

Amy's brain was muzzied by sleep. "Is it dinner time already?"

"No, my lady. It's 'is lordship. 'E came home in a proper snit demanding to see you at once."

"Very well. Help me put on the blue gown."

"There's no time, miss. You'd best go down in your dressing gown or 'e will be stormin' up 'ere to find you."

Amy wailed. "But what's happened? What have I done to anger him?"

"I don't know, miss. I only know I've never seen 'im so wrathful."

Amy ran the brush through the back of her hair

without bothering to use the mirror. She was tempted to call Aunt Charlotte but decided she must face Jason alone.

He was pacing the floor of the study when she entered. The ravages of his mood were written all over his face. Amy dropped a curtsy but he ignored it as he came toward her brandishing the broken sunshade. Instinctively she drew back against the wall and he stopped short a few feet in front of her.

"I've been told that you were in a carriage mishap in Hyde Park this afternoon. Is it true? Were you or Lady Charlotte injured in any way?"

Amy let her breath out slowly. "The carriage we were riding in sprung a wheel but neither Aunt Charlotte nor I were injured, nor was Captain Kinsgrove."

"Kinsgrove! The young puppy. I should never have permitted you to be escorted by such a fop. I'll wager the carriage was rented."

"Yes, I believe it was. However the accident was no fault of his. He was most skilled as a driver."

Jason's mouth curved with contempt. "You speak from a wealth of experience of course."

Amy smarted under the thrust. "One doesn't have to be in one's dotage, sir, to realize that a wheel caught in a rut is apt to be sprung. The captain made certain we were uninjured and saw that we had safe transport home."

"And just what manner of transport was it?"

"Private carriage, sir. A cabriolet, I believe."

"Belonging to whom?"

Amy brushed her hair back with exasperation. "To Mr. George Brummell."

Jason caught her chin in his hand, then tilted her head toward the light. "Good lord, you *have* been hurt. There's a bruise the size of a teacup on the side of your head." He brushed her hair back with a gentleness that surprised her, his anger having vanished as he became concerned.

She felt a weakness in her knees and she pressed her hands flat against the wall. Seeing the movement, he ordered her to lie down on the sofa next to the bookcase.

"Please, I'm perfectly all right. The bruise is nothing."

"Do as I tell you," he ordered as he yanked the bellpull and sent a servant scurrying for some herbal water. Pulling a chair up beside the couch, he looked at her closely. "Has the blow to your head affected your vision? Do you have a headache?"

"No. Truly, there is nothing amiss. I feel perfectly fit."

"Then why do you have tears in your eyes? You must be in pain."

Amy blinked rapidly but only succeeded in making the tears spill onto her cheeks. He took a square of linen from his pocket and blotted her face, his blue eyes dark with concern.

"You *are* in pain, aren't you?"

Her throat constricted, making it almost impossible to talk. "There is no p—pain. Y—you frightened me, Jason." It wasn't an absolute lie. He did frighten her but she would never let him know the true reason for her tears. When he touched her she felt a weakness so intense that it left her trembling and more vulnerable than she cared to admit.

His gaze softened as he reached for a copper curl and smoothed it over his finger. "I doubt that your fright was of any consequence compared to mine when I heard you had been injured. I left the club and nearly killed the horses in my haste to come home."

The servant arrived with the basin of herbal water and Jason placed it on the floor. Amy leaned up on one elbow.

"The club? But I thought you were with Lady Warrington tonight."

"Umm? No, not tonight." He put his hand on her shoulder and pushed her back against the cushions, then wrung out a square of lint and placed it against her head. She was terribly aware of his virility as he leaned close. She longed to reach up and trace the ridge of his cheekbone where it disappeared into the shadow of his hair. For a moment his gaze met hers and she paled, knowing that he could read every thought that crossed her mind.

93

CHAPTER SIX

Amy felt as if time had ceased to exist as Jason returned her gaze with ever increasing intensity. She knew that something was happening between them. She wanted to reach out to him but was afraid to break the spell.

At that moment Lady Charlotte tapped on the door and entered unbidden. She stopped shortly upon seeing them and pressed her palms together in front of her.

"What has happened here? What is going on, Jason?"

Jason jumped up quickly and stepped back like a schoolboy caught with his hands in the jelly pot. "I . . . we . . . uh . . . it's Lady Amy. I was just applying an herbal compress to the bruise on her forehead."

Charlotte strode over to give the wound a cursory inspection. "If this is the only complaint I think she needn't be concerned. At any rate, Jason, an herbal compress is hardly a cure." She looked down at Amy who still lay on the couch in her dressing gown with a liberal expanse of shapely ankle exposed to view. "It seems to me that perhaps more suitable attire would be of greater benefit to her present condition."

Amy got up quickly. "I'll change at once, Lady Charlotte." She ran from the room and didn't stop running until she reached the door of her bedchamber.

Polly, coming in from the sitting room, looked up in surprise. "Wot's this, miss?" she demanded.

Amy felt herself verging on hysteria. She wanted to cry but at the same time needed to laugh. Her words came out somewhere between the two. "It's nothing, Polly. Nothing's happened at all."

Polly murmured something about everyone gone crackers and proceeded to lay out the blue dress.

During dinner that night and for the following few weeks Jason was even more quiet and introspective than usual. Amy was well aware of his moodiness and frequent absences from the dinner table. She could only assume that he found it more relaxing to spend the time with Lady Warrington.

As each day passed Amy rapidly became the

95

center of a group of fashionable young men and women. Tuesdays were her "at home" days when she kept herself available to receive callers and the sun never set without at least a half dozen young bucks paying court to her. And not all of her suitors were young. Probably her favorite was Lord Andrew Graham, the Marquis of Melmoth, who had taken her to the concert at the Philharmonic Society. Amy liked his quiet good looks with the touch of gray at the temples. Furthermore she adored his three young daughters who often joined them for a stroll in the park.

Charlotte too was genuinely impressed with the man. Even more so when he gave her permission to examine his collection of rare Dresden china at his estate in Cadogan Square. Charlotte was so enthralled with the display of delicate miniatures that she hardly noticed when the marquis told her that he and Amy would stroll through the gardens. The children were visiting the farm in Chelsea with Miss Conroy, their nanny, and this was the first time in several weeks that Amy had seen him alone.

The marquis too seemed aware of the special circumstances as he reached for her hand. "My dear Amy, do you realize this is the first time we have been completely alone?"

She looked up at him and smiled. There was something so basically good and gentle that it seemed perfectly natural to permit him to hold her hand. "The gardens are lovely this time of year," she said. "I'm so glad that you brought me here, Lord Graham."

His fingers tightened on hers, though not uncomfortably so, and she sensed a certain tension in the air. He led her to a small open garden room surrounded by tall Ionic columns of white marble. In the center was a raised pool, the middle of which was covered by huge water lily pads and white waxy-looking star-shaped flowers. Amy was entranced with the tranquil beauty of the setting but when she looked at the marquis he seemed to be looking only at her.

"My dear Amy, I've wanted to bring you here since the night I first saw you at the Regent's gala. I wanted to see your reaction to my home" —he gestured with his free hand—"the house, the gardens, even my children. It suits you well and you must know that the children adore you."

Amy nodded. "And I them. They remind me so much of my sister students at the academy where I lived. They miss their mother. Even in their happy moments one can tell they are lonely." Tears sprang to her eyes and he looked contrite.

"Oh, my dear, I've made you sad. Please forgive me." He cupped her chin in his hand and lifted it to meet his face. When his lips found hers the touch was as gentle as a dove's wing brushing the autumn sky.

Amy caught her breath. It would have been an

97

untruth to say she didn't enjoy it, but good sense told her not to let him repeat his indiscretion. It was wrong for him to kiss her without first asking Jason's permission to pursue his courtship. She slowly gathered her skirts.

"I—I think perhaps it is best if we find Lady Charlotte, don't you agree?"

He looked greatly disturbed. "Only if you insist. Please forgive my boldness, Amy, but I find you quite irresistible."

She took his arm and they returned to the house. She had much to think about during the ride home. If truth be told she was somewhat disappointed in her first kiss. The thought crossed her mind that it was like a warm bath, soothing, relaxing, providing an overall feeling of contentment. But she had expected more. She had wanted her senses to be stirred until she was lifted above herself while her spirit soared. She smiled at her foolishness. Such romantic nonsense must have come from the French novel Miss Millicent Greaves hid under the bedcovers in the dormitory at St. Catherine's.

When the marquis had left in his carriage after seeing them home Lady Charlotte quizzed Amy about what had taken place in the garden and Amy told her. Lady Charlotte looked smugly satisfied.

"You couldn't have made a better conquest. The Marquis of Melmoth, in addition to his ancestral title, has holdings here and in Scotland. He has a reputation for being a careful man with his money, not like some of these young dashers who squander their fortunes at the gaming tables."

Amy remarked demurely, "He is an extremely nice man but he has made no mention of marriage. If he had I doubt that I could consider it. The most I feel for him is a deep affection."

"Dear heaven! Most marriages are begun on a far more tenuous thread than affection. You would do well to consider the matter before you decide. The man is much sought after and the time runs short for him to choose a wife if he hopes to sire a son."

Amy's face turned pink. "I'm sure we are concerning ourselves for nought. Lord Graham has yet to approach Jason for his blessing. I'm sure there are a dozen ladies with far greater expectations than I who would be willing to bear his sons. After all I have nothing to offer but myself. I could hardly expect Jason to provide a dowry after all he has done for me."

Charlotte, as usual, became flighty and nervous concerning the subject of money. She busied herself by searching through her reticule. "Yes, well, as you say, it is too soon to concern ourselves about an acceptance until you are spoken for." She pulled the strings taut. "What we really should be discussing is what we plan to wear to the rout at Penridge Castle."

99

Amy concealed her amusement with great difficulty. Aunt Charlotte was an expert at subterfuge but when it came to certain subjects she was as transparent as glass. Why the subject of Amy's past should completely unsettle the woman was something Amy was determined to find out.

The party at Penridge Castle was to be an afternoon affair extending into late evening, with some of the guests having been invited to stay the weekend. Amy and Charlotte were among those select few. Jason had declined due to press of business but planned to attend the first day as escort to Lady Warrington and her chaperon. Amy suspected that the real reason he refused to stay overnight was that Lady Warrington had been invited only for the afternoon and evening of the first day.

Several hopefuls had begged to escort Amy and her chaperon but in a moment of depression Amy decided to ride in the duke's carriage without benefit of escort. Surprisingly Jason permitted them the use of the State carriage while he settled for the more mundane cabriolet. Amy, with a twinge of uncharacteristic malice, knew full well that Lady Elizabeth Warrington would be less than pleased at riding second best. The thought gave a splendid lift to Amy's spirits.

By the time Amy and Lady Charlotte arrived at the castle most of the guests had already been settled into their rooms. Although Amy had been impressed by the size of Haddonfield Hall, it was nothing in comparison to the sprawling bulk of the ancient castle. They were met in the grand entrance hall by their hosts, the Duke of Thamesbrook and the Duchess Helene. Lady Helene, with her towering coif of smoky black hair that was encrusted with tiny diamonds, looked like she was born to the purple. She welcomed them with a warmth and sincerity that made Amy feel perfectly at ease. The duke, on the other hand, was a bit too effusive as his gaze lingered overlong on Amy's modest décolletage.

As for the castle itself Amy had never seen anything, except, of course, Carlton House, to compare with its magnificence. It was a combination of stark medieval with its ancient suits of armor and weaponry, and delicate, mystical fantasy with its allegorical murals and frescoes that ornamented the walls and ceilings. Thick Aubusson rugs in the colors of vintage wine were scattered generously over the stone floors.

The bedchamber to which Amy and Lady Charlotte were assigned in one of the turrets provided a sweeping view of wooded hillsides and valleys through the tall, narrow windows. To the left Amy caught a glimpse of the terraced lawn where a large group of people were amusing themselves at games while waiting for the luncheon to be served at a table set among the trees.

After giving her abigail, Marie, explicit instructions on how to care for their gowns, Charlotte saw that the woman was settled into her small cubicle adjoining the main bedchamber. Then she joined Amy at the window.

"Is it not magnificent? They say the castle was built in the time of William the Conqueror, the same as Windsor Castle. Point of fact I believe they are constructed of the same kind of stone. But come . . . we had best change before we join the party in the garden."

Lady Charlotte chose a petal-pink muslin with a wide band of cherry-pink satin at the slightly flared hemline. A necklace of diamonds and amethysts with a matching bracelet was the perfect complement. Amy wore a sea-green batiste with a slim, layered skirt cut in a scalloped design which added to her willowy look. A yellow silk rose tucked into the bodice hid the rather low décolletage. The yellow was repeated in a satin ribbon that formed a bow at the high gathered waist.

When they joined the group of people assembled around the long table that was now heaped with food Amy recognized several people. Beau Brummell, standing on the far side of the table, looked up from his conversation with a dark-haired beauty and lifted his glass. A few minutes later he had made his excuses and came toward Amy with an expression of eagerness on his face.

"Ah, Lady Dorset. I've been waiting for you to arrive." He smiled ruefully as it became apparent that others were moving in their direction. "Alas, it seems I am not the only one who has been waiting. Could I perhaps fix a plate of food for you and Lady Winford?"

Amy made a small face. "I fear I could not eat a morsel at present, but thank you, Mr. Brummell."

He bowed. "I'm disappointed, my lady, but I will forgive you if you will permit me to escort you and Lady Winford to dinner one evening in the near future."

"I'm sure both Lady Charlotte and I would be delighted." At that moment Amy was besieged by a group of gallants who vied for a position next to her. Lady Charlotte, a smug smile on her face, tactfully eased herself into the background but stayed close enough to hear most of what was being said. Amy was flattered by all the attention but one part of her kept stealing glances toward the stone porch at the central wing of the castle. Jason should have been here by now. Try as she would to not think about him, the day would not begin until he arrived.

A group of musicians began tuning up their instruments beneath a yellow canopy where a wooden floor had been laid over the grass to accommodate dancing. Two brave couples took the floor to demonstrate the latest dance sensation called the waltz. Most of the older people expressed genuine dismay at the immodest display as the dancers held each other closely in their arms. One diamond studded dowager fluttered her fan in haste as she commented in an acid voice. "Hmph! The King would never have permitted anything so immoral to be displayed in public. It's the Regent we have to blame for this. He's nothing but a pleasure-seeker."

Amy thought the dance looked graceful and quite romantic but wisely kept the opinion to herself. When a few more couples took the floor to learn the step Amy was invited but she declined. She did, however, dance the minuet with several young men.

Other games were provided to pass the time. A dart board was set up in the garden house and a number of people were avidly watching a dart game between two young officers. The contestants appeared to be enjoying themselves almost as much as those who shouted bets across the open room.

By early afternoon most of the people had wandered back to the tables which had been replenished with trays of cold meats, cheeses, crusty pork pie, fresh fruit marinated in wine, and flaky peach tarts topped off with thick Devonshire cream.

The Count Borelli, whom Jason had characterized as a bounder and a rake, kept their plates well filled and saw to it that their glasses were never empty. Privately Amy agreed with Jason's estimate of the man who frequently managed to brush against her as if by accident. She would be glad to have done with him.

It was much later when Jason still had failed to arrive and Amy, in desperation, turned to Lady Charlotte.

"I'm dreadfully concerned about Jason. Do you suppose he has had a mishap of some kind?"

Charlotte betrayed mild surprise. "I hardly think so. Lady Elizabeth has a penchant for making a dramatic entrance. She always makes it a point to be among the last to arrive." She shattered a tart with the tines of her gold fork. "I rather suspect they will appear shortly."

But he still had not arrived by the time the meal was over, and a short time later when it was announced that a cockfight would be held in the center of the dance floor, Amy was completely unsettled. The air had become quite warm and the guests a trifle on edge from having eaten too much and standing too long in the sun.

Those not interested in gambling on the cocks chose as an observation point the covered pavilion recently vacated by the musicians. The more vociferous of the gamblers made a semicircle around the floor as the hooded cocks were brought in. A table was set near the opening of the circle to hold a pitcher of iced lemon water and crystal goblets for those whose throats became parched from the loud shouting.

Count Borelli, eager to be in front, pulled Amy along with him while Charlotte took shelter in the pavilion. Amy was not feeling at all well. Her heart went out to the poor creatures who twisted their necks in blind anticipation as the voices of the gamblers grew even more raucous. Most of the wagers went to the black rooster whose feathers glistened with an iridescent green against the black. He looked eager to begin. The white rooster, smaller and more slender in the leg, seemed to smell death in the air.

Amy turned her head, refusing to become a part of the indecent display. She poured a glass of the lemon drink only to be jostled by the crowd as the spectacle began. It was impossible not to look as the flash of silver spurs honed razor sharp struck to kill. The shriek of pain as the rowel tore through feather to scrape bone was echoed by the delighted cries of the onlookers.

Each time blood was drawn the wagers increased and the cheers grew louder. Amy had begun to shake. The lemon water had soured on her stomach and she knew that if someone did not stop the carnage she was going to be ill.

Hardly aware of what she was doing she picked up the pitcher of lemon drink, ran to the center of the ring, and dumped the contents over the heads of the two fighting cocks. They broke away at once, shaking themselves in bewilderment as they uttered confused squeaks. The angry handlers tried to force them back into the ring but the fight had gone out of them.

Amy was immediately surrounded by the crowd of irate gamblers who fortunately did not physically harm her but subjected her to verbal abuse which was unfit for the ears of young ladies. She was close to tears. The fact that she had earned their displeasure did nothing to ease her embarrassment and she wanted desperately to get out of the unpleasant situation. She knew that Lady Charlotte would be trying to reach her side but there was little hope of that.

Only the backers of the white cock seemed to find the situation amusing. As one dandy put it, "A toast to the flamin' redhead who saved me a hundred quid."

But one of the backers of the black cock was indignant at having lost by default. "Who is that meddlesome gel, anyway? She reminds me of someone."

Another voice spoke up. "She's the daughter of Emily Concord, that's who. The actress who ran off and left her and the earl to travel the circuit."

"Then let's see if she can act. The doxy owes us something for spoiling our day."

Amy's eyes widened. "But I'm no actress. I've never been on the stage, except at school. Truly, I have never even been to the theatre."

A blond young man grinned down at her as he grabbed her arm. "Then we'll give you your first audition, my lady."

Amy sensed that half of the men were nearly foxed from an overabundance of wine. She would have to do something if she hoped to escape unscathed. She pushed firmly against the chests of the two men nearest her.

"Very well, if you insist on my making a fool of myself, I will do as you wish, but you must give me room to breathe."

The men let out a series of whoops and two of them ran to fetch another table while others dispatched the crystal goblets to the ground with singular disdain.

Lady Charlotte, having finally fought her way through the crush, was white around the lips. "Amy, for God's sake, you can't go through with this. Jason will be furious."

Amy tossed her hair back over her shoulders. "If he cared at all he would be here with us now instead of . . . of . . . Oh, never mind. It matters little what Jason thinks. It seems I have gotten myself into this and I will have to get myself out. Don't worry, Aunt Charlotte." She brushed a kiss against the woman's cheek. "I'll tell Jason you tried to stop me."

"As if that mattered. Really, Amy. You are courting disaster. This is a most unwise decision."

Amy nodded. "But it's my decision." Her eyes

108

opened in wonder. "It's one of the few things I've done on my own . . . and frightening as it is . . . it's a wonderful feeling."

The tables were fitted together and Amy put out her hands to a pair of young dashers who lifted her atop the makeshift stage. It was an incredible experience to look out over the group of nearly two hundred people who looked on in eager anticipation. She lifted her chin, smiled, and made a deep curtsy which resulted in a hearty round of applause.

Oddly enough it seemed they wanted her to succeed. That knowledge gave her confidence. She cleared her throat in an effort to steady her shaking voice.

"Oh, dear." She smiled. "What a pity I wasted all that lovely lemon water. I certainly could use some now." An observant lackey handed her a glass of champagne that she sipped and held aloft. "A toast to our feathered friends. May they enjoy the sweetness without the bitterness of the rind."

The crowd applauded her sly wit as she continued. "I know nothing of the theatre save what little I learned at the academy but I shall do my best to entertain you with a small speech from Shakespeare's *The Taming of the Shrew*. It is the final scene as Katharine speaks to Bianca and the Widow."

The gathering became silent as they strained

to hear her voice, strong, yet soft enough to set the mood and entice the listener.

"Fie, fie, unknit that threatening
    unkind brow,
And dart not scornful glances
    from those eyes,
To wound thy lord, thy king,
    thy governor. . . ."

She continued on, stumbling only once in her recitation until she came to the final line, "My hand is ready, may it do him ease."

They applauded her as if she had been on the stage at the Drury Lane. Amy knew it was out of kindness and perhaps out of respect for her nerve which held up well under the trying circumstances. She was laughing at an unabashed compliment from the man who was helping her down when she looked up and saw Jason striding across the green. His face was livid with pent-up rage.

Amy knew that he would be angry when he heard what she had done but she was hoping he would hear of it long after the deed had been accomplished. Trust fate to make him appear at that precise moment!

Jason shouldered his way with unconcerned roughness through the crowd of watchers. Grabbing Amy by the arm he nearly carried her across the green as he ordered a servant to summon his carriage. Charlotte, finding it nearly impossible to keep up with him, lifted her skirts to an unladylike degree as she scurried along behind.

"Jason, you must stop this. You are behaving with undue—"

His voice was deadly quiet. "I'll thank you to go to your room, Lady Charlotte, pack everything, and return to Haddonfield Hall at once. I'll see to it myself that Lady Dorset arrives home without getting into further trouble."

Lady Charlotte sighed in defeat as they approached the house. "Yes, Jason. Whatever you say." She looked at Amy and there was a veiled look of warning in her eyes.

CHAPTER SEVEN

Amy looked at Jason with fury born of humiliation. "Let go of me," she demanded. "Everyone is staring at us."

"Good. Perhaps next time you will think twice before making a spectacle of yourself."

"You're hurting my arm, Jason."

He eased off slightly but didn't loosen his grip until he unceremoniously shoved her into the carriage. To Amy's intense shame, Lady Elizabeth, in all her cool elegance, climbed in afterward, followed by her chaperon. Jason got in last and slammed the door with a look of apology to Lady Warrington.

"I sincerely regret these unfortunate circumstances, Elizabeth. If you prefer to stay on I can return later for you."

She looked at him from beneath demure lashes. "I wouldn't dream of inconveniencing you so, Jason, dear. The rout is unimportant compared with your . . . obligations." She slanted a look at Amy who felt her face burn with indignation.

The ride home was an endless nightmare. No one seemed able or willing to break through the heavy gloom that clouded the coach. As a result the miles were accomplished in almost total silence. Sitting on the seat next to Jason, Amy felt the rage emanating from him like a tangible force. She longed for the ride to be over, and yet she feared the inevitable confrontation when they were alone in his study. The full measure of his anger became evident when he told Lady Warrington that he would stop first at Haddonfield Hall and that he had given the driver orders to see that she arrived home safely. Lady Charlotte would have been horrified.

When they arrived home Jason leaped from the carriage instead of waiting for the footman to open the door, helped Amy down with no pretense of gentleness, and told her to go to his study. White-faced and shaken, Amy brushed past the footman and ignored Albert's concern. In the comparative safety of the study she sank down into a chair, endeavoring to make herself invisible. For a moment she imagined herself back in the office of the headmistress at St. Catherine's, expecting to see Mrs. Dupreen standing over her ready to strike with her heavy ruler. And so it was when Jason opened the door that Amy shrank back in fear.

He slammed the door shut with vehemence. "Must you cringe like that, Lady Amy? I don't plan to hit you, though by the saints you deserve it. But I'll tell you this, missy. We'll not have another scene like the one displayed today."

Seeing him alone, face-to-face, Amy took courage and mentally pulling herself together, stood up to confront him. The more she had thought about it the less she could see wrong with what she had done. If truth be told she would, if necessary, do the same thing again.

"I'm sorry, my lord, if I have displeased you." She saw the flint in his eyes and nearly wavered. Lifting her chin, she tossed her hair over her shoulder and continued. "I do not, however, apologize. Someone had to do something. Those poor creatures were being torn apart." Her voice quavered. "It would have gone on until one of them was dead if I hadn't thrown the pitcher of lemon water on them."

He looked at her in growing bewilderment. "In faith, Amy, I have not the slightest idea what you are talking about."

"Wh—why the cockfight, of course. I stopped it. Isn't that why you are so angry?"

"You poured a pitcher of lemon water over the fighting cocks?"

"Yes, my lord."

He put his hand to his face and partially turned away. "I can see how that would do it but I gather you managed to incur the wrath of those who had placed their wagers?"

"I'm afraid so."

"That hardly explains why you saw fit to behave like a hussy, making a display of yourself while everyone leered and applauded."

Amy bristled. "I don't think I made a spectacle of myself. True, they applauded, but I suspect the praise was for Mr. Shakespeare's words, rather for the manner in which I declaimed them."

"And what did you hope to gain? Was it your wish to call attention to the fact that you are the daughter of Emily Concord?"

"That was not my intention. I merely hoped to make amends for having spoiled the day's entertainment by dowsing the cocks." Her eyes blazed. "Furthermore I do not like the manner in which you refer to my mother. Although I do not remember her very well, she is, after all, my mother."

"She is also an actress, a profession which you should be aware is considered little better than being a courtesan."

Amy felt her face go white. "I assume, then, that you know her well."

"I have not seen her in many years."

"Then I would suggest, Lord Jason, that you are in no position to judge her. Indeed! I consider

115

it far more honorable to work for one's keep than to gamble away one's fortune and have to marry into money as most of the so-called gentlemen do."

Jason's face turned a fiery red above the snowy cravat. "We are not here to discuss your mother or the morals of the gentry. What concerns me is my duty to fulfill your father's wishes. Be assured they did not include permission for you to perform on stage."

"Tables," Amy corrected. "I would hardly compare it to the stage."

He caught her by the arm. "I warn you, Lady Amy. Don't bandy words with me." She winced at his grasp and he let go quickly. "And don't pretend I've wounded you."

"Then stop manhandling me. I have enough bruises for one day."

"Let me see."

"No, it's nothing, merely a tenderness from when you pulled me away from the tables."

He took her arm with a gentleness that belied his strength. "Yes, I see it has reddened and will no doubt turn blue. For that I beg your forgiveness."

Amy looked up in surprise and saw the pain in his eyes. "I assure you, it is nothing. I would prefer to forget about it and the entire incident."

He dragged his hand across his eyes. "Would that it were so easy." He looked down at her for several seconds, then clasped his hands behind his back as he strode across the room.

"It appears clear to me that I cannot in good conscience leave your total supervision in the hands of Lady Charlotte. Well-meaning as she is, she is far too permissive as judged by the standards set down by your father." He paused, flattening his palms on the surface of the desk. "Therefore I see no alternative but to severely restrict your social activities to events where I shall be able to accompany you."

"You make it sound as if I am to be a virtual prisoner in your home."

"Your home, too, Amy. And I would hardly call you a prisoner. Surely you will not have less freedom than you were accustomed to at Saint Catherine's?"

"But it will *seem* like less if I am confined to the house while you are away."

"Then I shall make every effort to share your confinement with you. Please understand that I have no desire to punish you. Nothing gives me greater pleasure than seeing you happy."

The warmth in his voice made tears sting her eyelids. She blinked rapidly to ward them off, then spread her hands in a helpless gesture. "It seems no matter how hard I try not to, I continue to be a burden to you. I am sure my father would not have wished it so and I can only beg your forgiveness, my lord."

He started toward her, then stopped abruptly as if meeting a solid wall. Amy thought he was going to reach out to her but he folded his arms across his chest. "Let us say no more about the incident." He opened the door. "If Lady Charlotte has returned I would like to speak to her alone. If you would be so good . . ."

Amy made a curtsy and he bowed in return. As she looked up their gaze held for an instant, sending a warmth flooding through her veins. She had come to the study expecting at the very least to be humiliated. Instead they had reached an understanding that gave her a feeling of security and well-being. Without even trying, she had extracted his promise to spend more time with her. True, a measure of guilt lay behind her satisfaction, but the joy she felt in having him near would compensate. She cared little for the parties and silly flirtations with the men of the beau monde. Her conquests meant nothing without Jason there to share them with her.

Amy was relieved that Jason wanted to speak to Lady Charlotte because it meant that she could postpone their scene for a time. For now, she wanted to be blissfully alone.

She lay on her bed for over an hour thinking about what Jason had said. It was foolish, this need to be near him. If she persisted in this childish infatuation she would only succeed in getting hurt, or worse, making a fool of herself. As Miss

Witherspoon at St. Catherine's had always said, "Any girl who pursues a man is destined to return with an empty game sack."

But am I pursuing him? What do I really want from Jason? Amy thought. She was saved from having to answer the question when a much subdued Lady Charlotte tapped on the door and entered the room.

Her voice was soothing. "My dear, I am so sorry it turned out this way. Jason has given his ultimatum and I fear there is little I can do to change his mind." She sat on the edge of the bed and patted Amy's arm. "But you mustn't fret. We shall manage until the duke returns and then we shall resume our little fling."

To please her chaperon Amy tried to look disappointed. "It was entirely my fault, Aunt Charlotte. You had everything arranged so perfectly but I seem to have spoiled your plans with my undisciplined behavior. I'm dreadfully sorry to have disappointed you."

"Disappointed? Nonsense!" She gave her a firm hug. "As long as you are not too heartbroken, nothing else matters." She brightened. "Did Jason tell you that he has about decided to take us for a visit to the country house?"

"No, he didn't mention it. Is it nice there?"

"Well . . . it's very quiet. Typical of the country, I suppose. Still, if we must go into exile I can't think of a better place. It will be at least a week

119

before he has his affairs in order so that he may leave, so in the meantime we shall have to make do with each other's company."

Amy returned her smile. "I consider myself to be the more fortunate on that score."

After Lady Charlotte had gone to her own room Amy reflected on how greatly she had come to care for her chaperon since they had first met in the office of the headmistress. Indeed Aunt Charlotte was closer to being a mother to her than her own mother had been since she had run off to join the traveling players. She wrinkled her nose. *Run off* was such a negative way to put it. Expressed that way, it made her mother seem even more irresponsible. And hadn't Lady Charlotte said that some people had a special calling? Amy felt the old familiar ache in the pit of her stomach. But if her mother had really loved her would she so easily have given her up? She pushed the thought to the back of her mind. For the present she lacked the strength to pursue it.

Jason was absent from the dinner table that evening and both Amy and Lady Charlotte retired early. Charlotte's abigail, Marie, had apparently wasted little time before relating the day's events to the servant grapevine. When Polly came in to help Amy undress her eyes held a new measure of respect for her mistress.

"Good lackaday!" she laughed, hugging her arms around herself. "I cawn't believe you really did it. No wonder 'is lordship stormed in 'ere like the devil on 'orseback. I'll wager 'e told you wot for."

Amy closed her eyes. "We did have a bit of a scene but I'd rather not talk about it."

"Never fret, miss. Whatever's happened is sure to look better in the mornin'."

But it didn't. Amy assumed that Jason would join her and Aunt Charlotte for breakfast but it appeared that he had not even returned home that night . . . nor did she see him all day. Much as she hated to admit it, Amy finally realized that Jason undoubtedly had taken the time to mend his fences with Lady Warrington. The more she thought about it the more despondent she became until the final insult when Albert informed her that his lordship would be dining out that evening. Amy knew the reason for her ill temper bordered on the ridiculous but she was unable to pull herself out of the gloom.

In an effort to cheer her up Polly selected a gown of amber chiffon which floated like a cloud over Amy's slender hips. It was far too extravagant for an evening at home but Amy didn't feel up to a discussion. Instead she sat quietly while Polly brushed her hair into a riot of curls which fell in a mass of radiance over her shoulders.

Charlotte voiced her approval when she took her place across from Amy at the long dinner table. "I'm pleased to see you looking better tonight, Amy. I was a bit concerned for you this morning."

Amy smiled. "The credit belongs to Polly. I'm afraid I have indulged myself in a bout of self-pity. In truth . . . I had almost decided to go without dinner this evening."

She had no sooner spoken the words than Albert bustled in with a fresh place setting that he laid out at Jason's chair. Lady Charlotte voiced the question Amy was dying to ask.

"Is Lord Jason dining at home after all, Albert?"

"Yes, mum. He will be downstairs directly."

Amy had to take a quick drink of water to calm her nerves. Lady Charlotte looked over the top of the low bowl of anemones that graced the table between them.

"If you have no objection, Amy, we might wait for the main course until Jason has joined us."

Amy nodded. To have tried to speak at this point would have been devastating. She only knew that in spite of her hunger she was in no hurry to eat.

Scarcely five minutes later Jason took his place at the table. He offered no explanation for his overnight absence nor did Lady Charlotte appear to expect one. He had taken time to change into soft gray breeches topped off with a burgundy velvet dinner jacket and a ruffled cravat in a light shade of pink. When the servant finished pouring the wine Jason unfolded his napkin and spoke.

"I hope I have not delayed your dinner overlong."

Charlotte waved her hand. "We chose to wait for you, Jason. You are looking well this evening. Do you plan to go out later?"

He looked up sharply as if trying to detect a note of criticism. "It is my intention to remain at home. There is something I wish to discuss with the two of you." He picked up the goblet and sipped slowly, much to Amy's irritation. Charlotte, too, betrayed her eagerness as she leaned forward while he laced his fingers together, resting his elbows on the table.

"I have learned that Elizabeth Billington is to be in concert tomorrow at Vauxhall Gardens. If it pleases you, I thought the three of us might have dinner there, then stroll through the gardens until time for the program to begin."

Amy sounded breathless. "How exciting! Are we actually going? Will there be fireworks?"

Jason smiled indulgently. "Of course we are going. As to the fireworks, the grand display is usually reserved for masquerade nights but there may be a small display of lights."

"Oh, Aunt Charlotte, please say you want to go."

"Of course I want to go. How considerate of

you, Jason, particularly when I know how much you dislike crowds."

"It is nothing, Aunt Charlotte. I did, after all, promise to make myself available as an escort until the duke returns to take over his duties."

Amy bristled. "I assure you, your lordship, that you needn't sacrifice yourself on my account. I have lived in seclusion before and I can survive the isolation until my legal guardian returns." She rose as if to leave the table. "I have no great desire to burden you with my company."

He looked at her through hooded eyes then drawled in a lazy voice, "Sit down, Amy. You are behaving like a child."

She smarted at the rebuke but did as she was told. The brief exchange had cast a pall over the evening that even Lady Charlotte's busy chatter failed to lift. Directly after dinner Jason excused himself and retired to his rooms. Lady Charlotte was so busy planning what they would wear that she didn't seem to notice that Amy was unusually quiet.

It was the next evening just prior to leaving for the gardens when Jason next appeared. Amy had been reluctant to go downstairs, but in a sudden show of defiance, she lifted her chin and gathered her skirts. She had given him a chance to back out. If he were so determined to play the martyr she might as well enjoy the concert to its fullest.

Polly had brushed her hair into a smooth coronet from which spilled a half dozen large curls like so many drops of molten copper. It was obvious from Jason's smile that he approved of her appearance.

He bowed low as she entered the room. "That particular shade of green is most becoming to you, Amy." He lifted an edge of material and smoothed it through his fingers. "It's soft, too, like the wings of a luna moth."

Amy caught her breath. She never knew what to expect from Jason. Was he simply being nice to make up for past slights? Lady Charlotte came in at that moment and he turned to greet her. A short time later they were on their way.

Amy had heard many stories about the famous Vauxhall Gardens but now, as she saw the hundreds of lanterns that lighted the entrance, she gasped in wonder at their splendor. The crowd was large because Elizabeth Billington was much in demand as a performer and tonight she was to sing *Merope e Polifonte* which was said to have been written especially for her by her Neapolitan lover Nasolini.

Having left the carriage, Jason gave each of the ladies an arm and guided them through the strollers to a series of boxes designed for intimate dining above the crush of the crowds. The boxes were arranged in tiers for alfresco dining among the tree tops.

Amy was so excited that she hardly knew what she was eating. Jason joined in the festive mood by making up amusing anecdotes to entertain them. Lady Charlotte was at her best; her biting humor at the expense of the unaware who paraded below sent Amy into gales of laughter. Jason tried to shame Lady Charlotte for her caustic wit but he finally capitulated and hid his grin behind a napkin.

Having eaten their fill of powdered beef, spiced fruits, cheese, crusty bread, and custards, Jason offered another round of syllabub laced with wine. Lady Charlotte held up a bejeweled hand.

"No more, Jason dear. I think it's time I switched to arrack punch or I shall be too tipsy to stroll in the gardens."

He lifted an eyebrow and grinned. "Remember, those were your words and not mine, Aunt Charlotte. We have less than an hour before the program begins. Would you like to walk through the garden?"

Amy looked pleadingly at Lady Charlotte who gathered her shawl. "A good idea. I think we could use the exercise after that divine meal."

As they mingled with the crowds who appeared to represent both the common class of people and the nobility, Amy saw several familiar faces. They waved friendly greetings but took one look at Jason and kept their distances. She was sure that people were talking about her behind gloved hands and fluttering fans but she admitted with some chagrin that she had brought it on herself by her scandalous behavior at Penridge Castle. Fortunately Jason appeared unaware of the gossip and it in no way affected his jovial mood.

They paused at the fountain and cascades to view the play of light on water and were pleasantly chilled by the spray that misted from the heads of fat marble cherubs.

Jason smiled warmly. "Since you seem to be enjoying this we shall have to return on masquerade night when over a thousand lanterns will be lighted. It is an unbelievable sight."

Amy reached over and squeezed his arm. "Truly, this is the most wonderful night of my life."

He looked at her in surprise, then returned the gesture of affection with a slight pressure of her arm against his side. For some several minutes Amy hardly felt her slippers touch the ground.

As they walked along an avenue of tall trees they came to a narrow pathway edged by towering yew hedges. It was too dimly lit to see inside, but when several young ladies entered the maze, one could hear a chorus of giggles and squeals broken occasionally by deeper voices. Amy looked up questioningly but Jason rushed them on past. Lady Charlotte refused to take the hint.

"That, my dear, is the Dark Walk where impudent young dandies wait to pursue the bolder of our young ladies."

Jason's voice was dry. "I would hardly call them ladies."

"But it's only harmless flirting," Lady Charlotte protested. "Have you never stolen a kiss behind the hedge on the Dark Walk?"

Amy felt Jason stiffen. "I would hardly consider it gentlemanly conduct, nor should you advocate the practice in the presence of your charge."

Charlotte was too far under the influence of the syllabub to let that pass. She giggled. "Don't be stuffy, Jason. They say even the Regent himself stole kisses here in his younger days."

"That in itself should be sufficient argument against it."

Fortunately for them all they were joined at that moment by the Marquis of Melmoth and his three daughters. The children forgot their exquisite manners in their haste to be first in line to embrace Amy, and it was only the stern voice of their father that quieted them.

"Forgive my daughters, your lordship." He bowed in turn to Lady Charlotte and Jason. "I fear my girls have allowed their joy in seeing Lady Amy to upset their decorum."

Amy's eyes sparkled. "The joy is mine, too. What a perfect evening to have all of my favorite people around me. May we sit together at the concert?" she begged, looking up at Jason.

He frowned but before he could answer the marquis interrupted. "I can think of nothing that would please me more, however we have come just to dine and stroll in the garden. The concert hour is too late for the children." He turned to Jason. "I wonder, sir, if you might spare me a few moments of your time before we leave?"

Lady Charlotte snapped to attention. "Perhaps the children and Lady Amy would like to see the koi in the pool by the fountain."

Jason nodded and gestured to Lady Charlotte who herded the small group down the walk. Amy was mildly curious as she pretended to watch the antics of the goldfish while covertly watching the two men. Charlotte, too, stole secret glances in that direction. When Amy looked at her in unspoken question Lady Charlotte's eyes began to dance. Mystified, Amy looked again at the two men. The marquis, apparently carrying most of the conversation, looked a trifle embarrassed but there was an eagerness about him that reminded her of a small boy. Jason stood still and white-faced in the soft glow of the lanterns. They both turned at that instant and looked at her. Suddenly a muscle twitched in her stomach and she knew . . . she knew . . . she knew!

CHAPTER EIGHT

Lady Charlotte, watching Amy's face, lifted her eyebrows in a gesture of triumph and nodded at Amy's wide-eyed look of amazement. Feeling suddenly weak in the knees, Amy sat down on the stone coping which surrounded the fountain. Immediately one of the girls sat down on either side of her and she had to hold on to Sara to keep her from tumbling. Moments later they were joined by the men.

Lord Graham gathered his protesting daughters and told them to say good-night. Bowing to Lady Charlotte and Jason, he again expressed his apologies for disturbing them. Turning to Amy, he reached for her hand and brushed it with his lips in a bare whisper of intimacy. She recalled his kiss by another fountain and it was with great effort that she was able to keep her voice even as she bade him good-night.

They might as well have forgotten the concert. Jason was apparently not going to say anything until later but it wasn't necessary, for Amy knew that the marquis had asked permission to pay court. Although Lady Charlotte was highly animated and speculated between numbers on whether the Regent was seeing the attractive singer in her Falmouth home as the gossips said, Jason and Amy were too deep in their own thoughts to comment. Jason fidgeted through most of the concert and untactfully sighed with relief when it was over. The ride home was oppressively silent.

Once inside the entrance hall Jason gave his top hat over to a footman and turned to the ladies. "I wonder if I might see both of you in the study before you retire."

It was a command, not a question, and Amy stood with her hand on the newel as if she planned a quick exit. She didn't want to hear it! Couldn't it wait? A look from Lady Charlotte stopped the thought before it could leave her head. Amy turned with resignation and followed them down the hall.

Untying her small bonnet and twirling it by the strings, Lady Charlotte smiled up at them.

131

"Wasn't this a delightful evening? We must do it again soon."

Jason's voice was low and strained as he asked them to sit down and then strode across the room and came to an abrupt halt behind the desk. He ran the back of his hand across his mouth then turned to Amy. "I . . . uh . . . There is no easy way to lead up to this. . . . I . . . the Marquis of Melmoth has asked for your hand in marriage."

Lady Charlotte nearly leaped from her chair. "Dear heaven! Just when things were looking so unfavorable. I had thought he was only asking permission to pay court!" Her enthusiasm nearly bubbled over. "Amy, my dear, you couldn't ask for a more perfect alliance. The marquis has a title of his own, is disgustingly wealthy, and is quite presentable in every way. Surely you must be overjoyed?"

"I . . . am rather surprised, Aunt Charlotte."

Jason asked dryly, "Am I to assume that you lack Aunt Charlotte's enthusiasm?"

Amy's throat was so tight, it hurt to speak. "Lord Graham is an exceptionally nice gentleman."

"Yes," Jason agreed. "One could hardly call him a callow youth. I'll wager he is at least ten years older than I. Why, his hair has already begun to gray at the temples."

Charlotte voiced her disdain. "Surely you can't fault the man for that. Some men turn white in their twenties."

"And he has three children, one of them nearly as old as Amy."

"But Amy adores them and they her. Besides, Jason, he wants children of his own."

"Aye!" He gave his chair a vicious shove. "He admits a male heir to be of paramount importance. Without it the title would be lost. One can sympathize with him, I suppose."

Amy felt her heart sink. "And is this his reason for offering for me, Jason?"

His face turned light pink. "The marquis admits to an affection for you. I daresay the man is not so old that he finds no attraction in your youth and beauty."

Charlotte smiled. "Surely you can't question his feelings toward you, my dear. The man controls himself well but he gave good evidence of his attraction for you when he kissed you in the gazebo." She nodded at Amy's distress. "Yes, I saw you but I found it unnecessary to intervene."

Jason breathed an oath. "You permitted the man to maul her? Dear Lord, I would have called the man out!"

Amy jumped up. "Please. This is most distressing. The marquis did me no harm. He is gentle and kind beyond words."

Jason went white around his mouth and his voice was low and tight. "I'm sorry if I frightened you, Amy. I realize that Aunt Charlotte would never have permitted any harm to come to you. It is only that I . . ." He spread his hands and turned away.

Lady Charlotte folded her hands with determination. "Think, Jason. This is the chance of a lifetime for Amy. Would you rather hand her over to some rascal who would gamble away her for—"

Jason cut her off. "Charlotte. Be still for heaven's sake."

Amy was shocked at his rudeness. For all their disagreements she had never seen Jason treat Lady Charlotte with less than the greatest respect. The reprimand struck Charlotte to the bone and she seemed to grow smaller beneath her shawl.

He came around to where Amy stood by the door and put his hands on her arms as he held her equally firmly with his gaze. "Is it your wish, too, that I give my consent?"

Tears burned her eyes as she looked up at him. "I want what you want, my lord."

He stared at her for a long moment, then pushed her away as he swore softly. "If you mean by that remark that you are happy to obey my commands, I find that hard to believe, considering your previously outrageous behavior. What I want to know is your feelings for the man. Do you love him or do you hate him?"

The room was filled with a silence that nearly shattered the air as the two Winfords waited for her answer. Her hands trembled as she drew a deep breath.

"I . . . I do not hate him, Jason."

He stared at her for a full minute, then strode to the door and opened it. "I bid the two of you good-night!" He slammed the door shut before either of them could answer and they heard his footsteps resounding down the hallway.

Lady Charlotte let out an audible sigh. "In heaven's name, what brought on that outburst? I have never seen him in such a temper."

"Will you excuse me, Aunt Charlotte? I'm dreadfully tired."

"There, there, child. Don't fret. Jason will give his consent. I can promise you that. Just leave everything to me." Charlotte was still trying to soothe Amy when she left her at the door of her bedchamber.

Amy leaned against the cool wood, relieved to be alone with her thoughts and emotions. Jason had given her a chance to say what she wanted but she didn't *know* what she wanted. She felt a deep friendship for Lord Graham but marriage . . . ? That was a difficult question.

She recognized the need within herself for the security and stability of a real home. Jason and Lady Charlotte had done their best to make her feel that Haddonfield Hall was more than a stopping place between school and marriage but she never really felt that she belonged. Still, in all

135

fairness to them, shouldn't she do her part to hasten her marriage and relieve them of the legal obligation?

The room seemed to close in on her until, with a gesture of impatience, she flung open the small door and stepped out onto the balcony. Resting her palms against the railing, she looked down at the terrace below. Silhouetted in the moonlight she saw a figure of a man who could only be Jason. He sat against the railing with his feet placed firmly on the floor. A cheroot glowed in his hands, momentarily lighting his face. She had never before seen him smoke.

The distance between them was considerable but Amy knew that he was watching her, as he had to know that she saw him. They held each other by a ribbon of thought, too slender to communicate with words, but too strong to break. They stood there for perhaps ten minutes without moving. She felt somehow as if he were reaching out to comfort her, and for one giddy moment, she would have sworn she felt his breath upon her face. It was a time of healing. She closed her eyes and let the warmth spread through her veins.

The mood was destroyed in an instant when Polly stepped to the door. "So there you be, miss. Would you be wanting the bed turned down now? I'll help you wi' your dress whenever you've a mind."

After Polly had finished her work Amy went

again to the window but this time no ash glowed to mark the smoker's hand. She felt an unaccountable sadness that stayed with her through the night and invaded her dreams like mist drifting over the moors.

It was no wraith who shook her awake the next morning. Lady Charlotte, showing surprising strength, pulled at her arm until Amy grudgingly sat up.

Lady Charlotte, already carefully dressed, threw open the draperies. "Wake up, child. Dear heaven, what I wouldn't give to sleep like that."

Amy groaned at the bright sunlight that flooded the room as her chaperon went to the dresser for Amy's hairbrush. "Here, you had better see to your hair. Jason wants to talk to us at once."

"Before breakfast?" Amy asked stupidly.

"Yes, if you think you can survive that long," she drawled. "I have a premonition that Jason has decided to give the marquis his blessing. But you look so surprised. Surely you didn't think Jason would refuse? He is no one's fool, you know."

"I . . . I just . . ."

"Do hurry. I think you are still half asleep."

With Polly's help they managed a hasty toilette and dressed her in a becoming gown of white-and-yellow-striped cambric. Jason was seated at the desk when Albert announced them and he rose as they entered.

137

"Please sit down." He spoke gravely. "I trust you both slept well?" His glance lingered over Amy who flushed upon being reminded of last night's vigil. His voice continued, strong and determined. "I have reached a decision." Lady Charlotte sat straighter, a smile puckering the corners of her mouth. Jason silenced her with a look. "I am leaving in a few hours for the house in the country. Just a few minutes ago I despatched a messenger to Lord Graham informing him that I will be away for a month and will, at the end of that period, give him my answer."

Amy stammered. "I—but can we do that?"

Jason, studiously avoiding Lady Charlotte's gaze, rubbed his hand across his eyes. "I suppose that strict etiquette might require a more definite response . . . but confound it all, the man is no calf-eyed yearling with his first great romance that he can't stand the wait." Jason suddenly looked horrified at what he had said but Amy chose to ignore it.

"Are you then going alone to the country house?" she said.

"Hardly. You and Lady Charlotte will join me. Did you imagine otherwise?" He lifted his cool gaze to hers and Amy looked away in confusion.

Lady Charlotte groaned. "I suppose it is hopeless to try and change your mind but I assure you I am not eager to rusticate for a full month."

"What a pity, Aunt Charlotte. As I recall you

seemed to rusticate in rather grand style under the attentions of Squire James Covington. And as I hear it the man is still looking for a wife."

Lady Charlotte blushed like a schoolgirl. "You'll do well to mind your manners, Jason. My age if nothing else should command respect."

He gave her a quick hug. "You have no need to worry, love. But for now I think it best if you see to the packing. I want to leave early enough to arrive in time for a late supper."

Amy started to follow Lady Charlotte from the room but he put a hand on her shoulder. "Is this what you wanted?"

She nodded. "Thank you, Jason, for the extra time."

"I think we both needed it," he said and then stammered, "I—in order to make the proper decision, I mean."

"Of course. I'll like the country. Are there horses?"

"Most certainly. Do you ride?"

She shook her head.

"Then I shall have to teach you."

Amy flew upstairs to pack. He had given her the gift of time and for the present, it was the most wonderful gift imaginable.

Most of the packing had to be left to Polly and Marie who would travel in a second carriage the next day. Amy and Lady Charlotte selected what they wanted sent, then packed a small valise with things they would need before the abigails arrived. The house was in a flurry of excitement getting them ready for the unexpected journey.

Once on their way Lady Charlotte was unusually silent as the high-sprung carriage creaked through the outskirts of London and into the rolling countryside. Jason, who admittedly loved the country more than the city, looked years younger in his rugged twill breeches and coat. As for herself, Amy felt more carefree than she could ever remember having felt before.

When the carriage overtook a small dogcart loaded with baskets of chickens for the market the young driver looked up and waved, a goodly space showing between his teeth as he smiled. He was whistling a folk melody which Amy recognized and began to sing. Soon Jason joined in the song with his deep basso and began to clap in time to the rhythm.

Lady Charlotte looked most astounded by their apparent good humor as she listened without comment. When they had gone through several rollicking tunes she motioned to Amy.

"Move to the other side, dear. I think I shall stretch out and doze for a while."

Jason, who sat facing them, moved to the side and attempted to compress his long legs into a smaller space. When Amy stumbled against him as she moved across the aisle he reached to steady her arm and the touch of his fingers remained long after he had taken his hand away. She was dreadfully aware of his nearness as she watched the interplay of muscle against bone as he drummed his fingers along the window frame. Dark hair curled against hard knuckles, contrasting sharply with the narrow white moons of his closely pared fingernails. *He smells clean,* she thought, *and very, very masculine.*

Sitting this close together, they were unable to resume the easy camaraderie they had experienced before. There was an unexpected awkwardness until Amy asked him to tell her about Winford Farms.

"Is it really as rustic as Lady Charlotte says? Will I be required to milk cows?"

He grinned. "Do you know how to milk cows?"

"No, but you can teach me."

"I'm not sure that I remember how. It has been years since I have had time for that kind of work."

"You grew up there?"

"Yes, as did generations of my family before me. The country house was built on land granted to the Winfords by Queen Elizabeth who decreed it a duchy."

"It doesn't sound countrified to me."

"I'm reasonably certain you will find it comfortable, but if you are hoping for a continuous round of parties and wild routs, you will doubtless be disappointed."

Amy wrinkled her nose. "I've had a sufficiency

of parties for a while. After all, I did not manage too well at the last one."

He chewed his lip in an obvious attempt to hide a smile. "It can never be said that you are a wallflower. You always seem to draw your share of attention."

Amy nodded. "It's my hair. The headmistress at Saint Catherine's said it was the root of my problems, including my temper. At one point she threatened to shave my head."

Jason gazed at her as a smile played at the corners of his mouth. "To cut your hair would have been a crime worthy of transportation to the Colonies."

"Thank you," she whispered, then turned quickly to hide her face as she pretended to watch the passing scenery.

It was nearly an hour later when Lady Charlotte roused herself. "Dear me, I slept more soundly than I had expected. We must be nearly there. Isn't that Squire Dennison's place?"

Jason nodded, then leaned close to Amy and pointed out her window. "We will be at the house in just a few minutes. Yonder, through the growth of alder trees, you can see the chimneys of Winford Farms. In truth the boundaries of the ducal grant began some distance back at the great stone markers that bore the family crest."

Amy caught her breath. "Do you mean that all this land belongs to your family?"

He laughed. "This and much more. Our holdings include meadows, streams, a small lake, a deer park, and even a good portion of the village that lies just beyond the mansion."

Amy looked at Lady Charlotte and laughed. "And this is what you called rusticating?"

Lady Charlotte yawned. "I was referring to the provincial society, not the accommodations. Just wait until you ask your abigail to do your hair. The local girls hardly know the difference between a hairbrush and a horse's currycomb."

Jason spoke dryly. "I'm sure you can manage until your maids arrive. After all it is not as if we will be dressing for Carlton House."

"My point exactly, Jason, my dear. One hardly has to dress up to please the farm animals, does one?" She was immediately contrite as she reached over to pat his hand. "Don't worry, my love. We shall manage. I'm sure it will do us all good to get away from the stench of London and breathe some fresh air."

The carriage passed through a great iron gateway next to a small, immaculately kept cottage, then continued on down a lane which was bordered on each side by towering elm trees whose branches laced together overhead to form a canopy. As they neared the great house the drive followed a serpentine course that was bordered by a yew hedge trimmed in the topiary style of a crenellated battlement.

Although the sun had set an hour ago, there was still enough light for Amy to clearly see the house. It was stone: gray fieldstone mellowed to a warmth possible only with age. The center section dated back to Tudor times, Jason pointed out, while the less ancient stonework was softened by a curtain of ivy that curled against mullioned windowpanes. It was a house of many levels and angles, rather than the clean, straight lines which personified Haddonfield Hall. Some people might have considered the architecture too fanciful or, put more kindly, romantic, but Amy found it altogether delightful.

As the carriage pulled to a stop at the terraced entrance Amy discovered another difference. In London the staff would have sprung to attention, but here, it was only after the coachman had pulled the bellrope that the footman appeared to assist them.

Jason went ahead up the low terrace steps to the enormous oak doors that stood invitingly open. Lady Charlotte followed but Amy lingered behind to savor the beauty of the house and grounds. Strangely it all seemed so lovingly familiar to her. Had she visited here as a child or was this simply the embodiment of a childish fantasy of the house in which she would like to live?

Just inside the door, Harrison, a butler of an-

144

cient vintage, bowed his snow-white head in rheumatic awkwardness. He took her shawl and spoke with a strength which belied his infirmities.

"Welcome home, Lady Amy."

CHAPTER NINE

"Welcome home!" No one had ever said that to her before and it echoed and reechoed through her head even as she prepared for bed. She wanted desperately to feel as if it were home but in her heart she knew it was only temporary.

A buxom middle-aged maid was called upon to assist the women with their personal needs until their own abigails arrived the next day. She was too well trained to offer any but the most polite conversation but she blossomed considerably when Amy commented favorably about the appearance of her bedchamber.

In this room, like most of the other rooms Amy had seen at Winford Farms, there was an almost tangible feeling of warmth and comfort. Where

146

Haddonfield Hall gloried in its polish, elegance, and glitter, this house nestled to the earth, with its huge beamed ceilings and its heavy oak furniture designed for comfort rather than display. The colors were of the earth's harvest: browns, greens, gold, tangerine, and pumpkin. That wasn't to say the house was less nice than Haddonfield Hall, it was the mood that was different. She smiled to herself. The town house furniture with its delicate spindle legs would be as out of place here as the sea chest which stood beneath her window would be in the grand foyer in London.

Even the sounds were different here. In London one could hear the screech of carriage wheels long after midnight announcing the coming home of noisy revelers. Here, however, the staff retired early and rose with the dawn to meet the demands of a working estate. And yet somehow the pace was more relaxed here in the country and Amy knew she would like it.

When she awoke the next morning Amy wondered where she was. A light breeze lifted the ruffled chintz curtain providing a glimpse of dappled sunlight filtering through the green-and-white velvet leaves of a poplar tree. The sun was already high in the sky. She felt a twinge of guilt at having slept so long and quickly swung her legs over the edge of the high four-poster bed as she gave a pull on the bellrope. When the maid arrived she selected a green-and-white cotton dress with a white lace fichu and hurriedly finished her preparations.

Lady Charlotte and Jason had long since finished their breakfast, while Amy's was being kept warm for her on the huge sideboard.

She helped herself to a generous serving of porridge that was kept hot over a candle burner, adding a thin slice of fine white bread sparingly spread with butter and apricot conserve. Harrison, bringing in a hot pot of tea, informed her that Lady Charlotte and Jason were waiting for her to join them at the carriage house for a tour of the estate.

Jason had chosen an open park phaeton so they might ride through the countryside with an unobstructed view. Although Lady Charlotte pretended boredom with the idea, Amy had the feeling that she was hiding her true feelings. Jason was plainly eager to begin the tour.

They turned south down the drive, then crossed a narrow bridge over a rushing stream which Jason said provided fresh water for the great house, the farm, and most of the village. At one point the stream had been dammed to form a large pond which had been stocked with perch. It was obvious that Jason was nearly bursting with pride.

Lady Charlotte was equally as proud of Jason. "What he hasn't told you, Amy, is that it was his idea when he was fourteen to build the dam and stock the pond with fish. His foresight saw the village through a time of famine when many people might have gone hungry had it not been for the fish. The willow trees that he ordered planted along the stream have provided osier rods for the baskets, carriage bodies, and willow furniture used in the village."

"But I thought most cottage crafts had become industrialized and had moved to the city," Amy said.

Jason shrugged. "That's true, for those who live near the city found they could make more money in the manufactories, but the farther one travels from the city, the more home crafts one can find. For example: our women still do their own weaving and spinning. Our men still work the farms but in addition they supplement their income by clockmaking, chandlery, carpentry, or whatever skill they possess."

Lady Charlotte agreed. "Some people call it the half-and-half way of eking out a living."

As they drove into the village laborers dressed in durable fustian trousers doffed their caps to welcome Jason and his party. The women, dressed in dark cotton with white mobcaps or bonnets pulled carefully over their hair, curtsied in apparent pleasure at seeing Jason after his prolonged absence. It was the children in particular who impressed Amy. Contrasted to the thin, sickly looking child of the London streets, these youngsters radiated robust health. They ran after the carriage laughing and shouting with complete lack of respect for the nobility. Amy was grateful that Jason not only tolerated their effervescence but was delighted by it.

As they neared the small church with its ancient stone wall and white steepled bell tower, Jason told the driver to pull up alongside the two gentlemen who stood talking near the gate. When Amy noticed the sudden flush that colored Lady Charlotte's face, she took a second look at the two men. One, short and paunchy, was obviously the vicar. The other was a tall, dignified-looking man with skin browned to an even tan and a thatch of incredibly white hair. While his complexion suggested a man of the soil, his well-cut tweed coat and trim breeches over sleek, Hessian boots depicted a man of quality.

Lady Charlotte fidgeted with her bonnet as the carriage stopped and the two men strode over to meet them. After an exchange of greetings the white-haired man placed his hand on the framework of the carriage, daringly close to Lady Charlotte's arm.

"I say," he spoke in a deeply resonant voice. "This is a dashing good surprise, Lord Jason. You have been away much too long." But while he spoke his gaze never once left Lady Charlotte's face.

Jason smiled. "You're looking fit, Squire Covington, and you also, Vicar. I agree, it's been far too long. May I present my father's ward, Lady Amy Dorset? Squire James Covington and the Reverend Fletcher."

Squire Covington bowed again. "Am I to assume that you are the daughter of the late Earl of Concord?"

Jason cut into the conversation. "That is true. Since this is her first trip to the country we are most eager for her to see the sights."

Although it was apparent that Jason wanted to move on, the squire would not let him leave that easily. He fastened his gaze once again on Lady Charlotte and extracted a promise from her that she would join him for a tour of his garden the following morning. Somewhat as an afterthought he included Amy in the invitation but a sixth sense made her decline. As they pulled away Lady Charlotte scolded her. "Really, my dear, it would have been more polite to have accepted."

"But I thought the squire was only asking me out of generosity. I'm sure he wanted to see you alone."

"Nonsense! I've seen the garden dozens of times."

Jason laughed heartily. "You know as I do, Aunt Charlotte, that the rose garden was merely a ploy so the good squire can get you alone to hold your hand and whisper endearments."

Lady Charlotte glared and tossed her curls.

151

"Don't be ridiculous, Jason. You talk as if he were a lovesick boy."

"He isn't a boy anymore but I doubt that he has spent all his youthful passions."

Lady Charlotte glanced sideways at Amy. "Enough of this. You forget yourself, Jason."

He flashed a smile at Amy who dimpled in delight at having been included in the conspiracy to enjoy her chaperon's discomfort. She lifted her face to the sky and felt her heart overflow at the wonder of belonging to all this. It gave her such a feeling of contentment that she was sure no earthly power could dispel her inner joy.

As they passed through the village Jason pointed out the shops of the smithy, the carpenter, and the rope maker, but Amy, riding along in a state of euphoria, just barely managed to make the proper responses.

As they passed into the poorer section of the village some of the people paused to look up but few of them waved or even smiled. Lady Charlotte pointed out that they had left the boundaries of the Winford holdings and had entered the perimeter of Mare's Run.

Amy followed her line of vision and saw an arrow-straight lane surrounded by a low wooden fence that led to a darkly imposing mansion unsoftened by trees or shrubbery.

"It looks so cold and unloved," Amy said. "I'll bet it has an underground dungeon."

Lady Charlotte chuckled. "It would be wise not to let Lady Elizabeth hear you say that."

"Lady Elizabeth?"

"Warrington," Jason supplied. "Mare's Run has been in the Warrington family for generations. There are those who say it was a prison at one time before it fell into the Warrington line."

Amy was almost afraid to ask the next question. "Does Lady Elizabeth ever come here to live?"

Jason crossed his knees. "Actually she almost never comes here, since she prefers the social activities of London. However, it is my understanding that she will arrive tomorrow for an extended visit."

Lady Charlotte sniffed. "Only for as long as you plan to be here, I'll wager."

"Really, Aunt Charlotte, I'm sure she has a better reason."

Amy doubted it but she was too wise to comment. She sighed aloud and Jason looked at her.

"Are you tired, Amy? I had forgotten about our long ride yesterday. Perhaps you would prefer a rest or a stroll in the garden?"

"No, I'm perfectly fine, thank you."

Lady Charlotte fluttered her fan. "Well I, for one, would like to return to the house. If Marie and my trunks have not arrived I shall be in dire straits for something to wear to the squire's house tomorrow." She patted Amy's hand. "My dear, I hope you will forgive me for deserting you so soon

153

after our arrival. Such a dreadful nuisance, but it would have been awkward to refuse." Amy had to hide her smile behind a yawn as Lady Charlotte continued. "What will you do to entertain yourself while I am away?"

Jason cleared his throat. "I thought perhaps we might begin her riding lessons."

Amy's eyes sparkled. "Do you really mean it? I've always wanted to learn to ride."

Jason assured her that they would begin the next day. Later, though, in her bedchamber, Amy began to worry over the prospect of learning to ride. Lady Charlotte, having planted her small frame in a rocking chair, scrutinized Amy's face.

"Judging from your face, I would rather imagine you are experiencing some discomfort about your riding lesson tomorrow. Since you have no aversion to horses, I can only surmise that you are averse to having Jason teach you."

"It is only that I'm afraid I shall make a fool of myself."

"Nonsense! Riding is not difficult if you have a proper mount and Winford Farms has some of the best." She stretched out her short legs and set the chair in motion. "Just don't let Jason bully you. He is something of a perfectionist, and being inclined toward the overly cautious, he will no doubt try to keep you forever within the confines of the paddock."

"I suppose it would be much safer there."

They heard a carriage drive up and Amy went to the window to see who it was. "It's Polly and Marie arriving in the coach with our luggage."

"Mercy!" Lady Charlotte popped out of her chair. "I would never have believed I would miss my abigail so much, but one day more of having the country bumpkin do my hair, and I would go bald."

Polly was as happy to be in the country as Amy was to see her. Amy had become quite fond of the bubbly, unpretentious maid who was so close to her own age.

"Great lackaday!" she exclaimed as she circled Amy. "Wot can these rustics be thinking of? I declare, miss, they've let you wear your dress straight from the valise. Take it off, Lady Amy, and I'll 'ot up my iron."

Amy told her that it would do until time to change for tea, but she hastened to add how much she had missed Polly and was glad she had arrived safely.

If the first full day in the country were any indication, Jason would be spending a great deal of time at home. He seemed to be more relaxed and happy here than at Haddonfield Hall and Amy was ecstatic. Both Polly and Lady Charlotte commented on how the fresh country air had brought a sparkle to Amy's face.

The afternoon was spent getting the maids settled in and helping them unpack the trunks and

155

organizing the armoires. Jason, with very little protest from Amy who felt guilty about leaving the work for Lady Charlotte, had whisked her off for a grand tour of the mansion and its treasures. He took special pride in telling her about his predecessors and their influences, both good and bad, upon the country. When it came to the various collections of artifacts and paintings, he was quite knowledgeable about their origins and how they were obtained.

After dinner that evening the three of them took their coffee in the low-ceilinged library with its dark-paneled walls. Although a fire seemed unnecessary this time of year, Amy soon found that it added a coziness to the room, as it took away the dampness. In addition she soon learned that the real reason Jason wanted a fire was to pop corn. He knelt on one knee and shook the wire basket over the coals as he grinned up at Amy.

"I haven't done this since I was ten years old and yet I feel as if it were yesterday."

Amy curled up on the floor beside him and gazed into the embers. "It seems so strange to be here. When I was a child at Saint Catherine's, I used to lie awake at night and dream of being a part of a family and doing things like this, but I really never expected it to happen."

Jason gripped her shoulder with his free hand. "I'm sorry for all your childhood unhappiness, Amy. I wish I could make it up to you."

She leaned back and looked up at him, her hair falling in a copper cascade down her back. "But you have, haven't you? You've given me more happiness than I've had in all my years put together. Had not the duke been appointed my guardian I would probably still be at Saint Catherine's or looking for a position as a nanny to someone's children."

"I assure you, that would never have happened." He rose abruptly and emptied the popcorn into a bowl while Lady Charlotte melted a pan of butter over the fire.

"Don't underestimate your father, Amy. He may have seemed cold and uncaring but he was a warm, loving man who never would have left you unprovided for."

A dark look passed from Jason to Lady Charlotte and she laughed a little hollowly. "But why are we being so maudlin? Play for us, Amy. Something we can sing together."

She seated herself at the pianoforte and ran her fingers over the keys before drifting into the familiar strains of "Maids in the Heather and Sheep on the Hill." Jason joined his deep voice with Amy's clear soprano as Lady Charlotte surprised them by adding her strong alto for a pleasant three-part harmony.

Amy was all too aware of Jason's nearness as he brushed against her shoulder. As he turned the page his arm all but encircled her and she momentarily lost her place. She prayed that no one noticed the added quaver to her voice.

It came as a surprise when Jason drew his timepiece from his pocket and shook it to be sure it was running. "I had no idea the hour had grown so late. If we are to meet at the stables in the morning we should retire soon." He drew himself up and made a formal bow. "My compliments to the two of you for making our homecoming one of the most delightful I have ever known."

Lady Charlotte and Amy were quiet as they climbed the stairs. Amy, for one, was afraid she would break the spell that held her in this fragile web of happiness. She dispensed with Polly as quickly as possible, then settled between the sheets with the hope that her dreams would take up where the evening had left off. Unfortunately her last waking thoughts were of the riding lessons set for the next day. Her unconscious mind, perhaps remembering what Lady Charlotte had said about Jason being a bully, clouded her dreams with ugly thoughts. Luckily, though, they seemed without foundation when she awoke.

In truth when Jason met her at the stable the next morning he seemed to be the epitome of gentleness, both with her and the horses he chose for them to ride. His was a huge black stallion named Mephisto. Judging from the way he arched his neck and pawed the ground, Amy thought he was well named. Her horse was a placid creature

158

with limpid brown eyes and a dappled brown coat that reminded Amy of autumn leaves touched with frost. Ysobel responded willingly to the slightest pressure on the rein and a gentle word of direction.

The first day Jason insisted that they merely walk the horses until she learned the basic posture and use of the hands and legs. By the time Jason put an end to the lesson Amy had begun to feel a dull ache in the small of her back from the unaccustomed sidesaddle position. Nevertheless she felt an overpowering urge to ride after him when, after seeing her horse turned over to the groom, he sent his horse over the rail and galloped toward the road. To make matters worse the direction he chose was that of the Warrington estate. Amy's only consolation was that he had promised another riding lesson the following morning.

Lady Charlotte still had not returned by teatime and Amy, feeling rather odd about being alone for the first time, took tea in her room. She spent the time working on an embroidered shawl which she planned to give to Lady Charlotte.

When Lady Charlotte returned sometime later it was with the news that Jason would not be home for dinner. A pall settled over the day but it apparently in no way affected Lady Charlotte whom Amy had never seen looking so vibrantly alive. As they dined together in the comfort of their shared sitting room, Lady Charlotte put her cup down with an unusual lack of grace.

"Amy, dear, you have been staring at me since the moment I returned to the house. I'm beginning to wonder if something is amiss. Is my hair in disorder?"

Amy shrugged. "Actually the reverse is true, Aunt Charlotte. I was just thinking how perfectly marvelous you look since we came to the country."

Lady Charlotte turned a bright pink. "I strongly suspect that Jason has been prompting you. For five years he has been trying to convince me to accept the squire's proposal of marriage."

"I . . . I have often wondered why you never married," Amy began timidly. "As attractive as you are you must have had dozens of offers."

"None that meant anything to me. The man whom I wanted to marry found that he loved another woman more than he loved me."

"The man who gave you the brooch?"

"Yes."

"And you still hope to marry him one day?"

Lady Charlotte stared at Amy as if she were looking straight through her. "No, child. It's too late for that now. The man was your father."

Tears sprung quickly to Amy's eyes as she reached across the table to touch Lady Charlotte's hand. "Forgive me for prying, Aunt Charlotte. I had no idea."

Lady Charlotte returned the pressure. "It's

quite all right. I should have told you long ago but never found the proper moment."

"But you waited for him all those years. Why didn't he marry you after he and Mother were divorced?" Amy realized too late the tactlessness of her question but Lady Charlotte appeared not to notice.

"Your father never guessed how much I cared for him and it would have been improper for me to make an advance. In truth I think he still loved your mother despite their vast differences in how they chose to live."

"But how could he love her when she left us to join the theatre? She couldn't have loved us to any great degree."

"Don't be too harsh, Amy. It's hard to know what lies in another's heart."

"But you've waited all these years for a man who never came to you. Surely you owe it to yourself to find some measure of happiness in the years ahead. It's my guess that you are more fond of the squire than you care to admit."

Lady Charlotte adjusted her fichu with nervous fingers. "Of late I have been having the same thoughts. Perhaps, my dear, when we have you safely and happily established in your own home, I shall give the good squire the surprise of his life and accept his offer." She lifted the teapot from its quilted cozy and filled their cups. "Which brings to mind your own indecision regarding

Lord Graham's offer for your hand. Have you and Jason had an opportunity to discuss further a possible alliance between you and the marquis?"

Amy shook her head. "He hasn't mentioned it since we came to the country . . . nor have I."

"I take that to mean you are somewhat cool toward the idea or you would be pressing your case."

Amy realized later that she had detected a note of disappointment in the woman's voice. She pondered the reaction as she lay in bed and stared at the pleated canopy overhead. *But of course Aunt Charlotte had been disappointed! Hadn't she intimated that she was only waiting for me to get settled so that she could plan her own marriage?*

She had come to love Aunt Charlotte as a mother in the short time she had known her. Indeed, except for a quirk of fate, Lady Charlotte might have been her mother. *Surely it must be up to me to do everything in my power to make Aunt Charlotte happy*, thought Amy. *If I accept the marquis's proposal it would solve so many problems, but can I go through with it? Can I marry him?*

A short time later she heard Jason enter the house, no doubt after spending the evening with Lady Warrington. And he was whistling! Amy clapped her hands over her ears and buried her head in the pillow.

CHAPTER TEN

Jason, looking more fit and handsome than ever in his buff whipcord riding breeches and brown tweed jacket, was waiting in the paddock with the horses already saddled when Amy got there. He had been pleased with her progress in learning to ride the past few days but he was still unwilling to let her venture beyond the confines of the paddock. She had taken special care with her appearance this morning in the hope that she could convince him to take her riding with him through the open meadows and woodland. Being restricted in her social life was one thing, but now that she had mastered the art of staying in the saddle and controlling her mount, she felt he was unnecessarily strict.

She smiled happily when she saw his look of approval at her new costume. The divided skirt of pale blue velvet swirled around her legs in a fetching manner. The fine white kid boots matched the white kid gloves and white straw bonnet with its long blue ostrich feathers which was a gift from Aunt Charlotte. It was a lovely outfit, but if truth be told, she would have rather stripped to shirt and breeches and swung her legs astride as the men did.

Jason made a semblance of a bow. "How smashing you look this morning. Is that a new riding costume?"

She twirled around, unconsciously showing off her slim figure and rounded curves. "Yes. This is the first time I have worn it. I thought perhaps we might ride through the deer park today." She flashed her most winning smile.

Jason grinned. "I suspected an ulterior motive but I think it would be wise to have a few more lessons before we attempt the trails. There is some rugged terrain beyond the gates and the horses have not had as much exercise as they should have."

She pulled a face at him, causing him to grin harder as he tightened a cinch. "Why all the hurry? We have plenty of time for you to try the woodland trails before we return to London."

"Aunt Charlotte was right. You are a bully."

"I prefer to think of myself as a stern teacher."

164

He gave her a hand onto the saddle and offered her the reins. "Today we will concentrate on the various paces, after which we will try the low and intermediate jumps. You still have a tendency to slouch. Remember to keep your elbows in and your back straight as you lean forward."

Ysobel responded more quickly than ever to the commands Amy gave her. The gentle brown-eyed horse seemed eager to please as she moved restlessly, waiting for the ride to begin. Amy echoed her restlessness. She was tired of the paddock and the mundane paces and longed to follow Jason along the paths in the forest. It seemed like no time at all when he told her the lesson was over for the day. Seeing her obvious disappointment, he told her that he would ask the groom to saddle a horse and ride with her inside the paddock. When he turned his mount and headed toward the stables Amy dug her heels into the mare's flanks and galloped toward the fence. For one dreadful moment she thought the horse would refuse the jump, but Ysobel lowered her ears and sailed over the rails in one silken motion, landing as perfectly as if the jump had been rehearsed. Amy's hands were shaking at her own temerity but she exulted in her fear. Turning the horse toward the meadow, she set her gaze on the woodland, away from the trail that led to the Warrington estate.

She could see ahead of her an opening in the

165

dense stand of pine trees. There were no fences to bar her way and so nothing would stop her. Indeed the horse had taken her head and Amy was uncertain if Ysobel could be stopped until after she had run her fill.

Moments later she heard the pounding of hooves following behind her. Jason had come after her as she knew he would, but she wasn't about to give in yet. A quick glance told her that he was much angrier than she had predicted. He was waving his cap with a motion that emphasized the fury written on his face. Amy knew that it was foolish to go on but she wanted desperately to have her own way just this once.

The path was climbing now and was edged with boulders along one side. The sound of the horse's hooves was muffled by the carpet of pine needles that covered the trail but Amy could hear Jason's horse gaining on them from the rear. Ysobel was tiring. Amy didn't have the heart to use the whip. The mare was no match for Jason's powerful stallion. It was just a question of minutes until he would reach them. She swallowed, fighting the panic that threatened to overwhelm her. Jason was in a rage; even from this distance it was all too clear.

Suddenly she laughed a high, ringing sound that echoed down the path. She wanted him to be angry! The thought of having enough power over him to evoke such rage sent a surge of heat through her veins and she laughed again. There was a wildness inside her that she never dreamed existed. It was the thrill of the chase that had set it free and she exulted in it.

He was gaining rapidly. The mare's sides heaved as she set her teeth against the bit and dug her hooves into the soft turf. Amy bent low in the saddle to avoid the overhanging branches. Her hat had long since fallen and her hair streamed backward like a red banner waved before a charging bull.

He was only yards behind her now, no longer shouting. His mouth was set in a thin line which cut like a scar across his face. In one quick glance Amy saw again the eyes of the hawk as he fastened his gaze upon her. She sucked in her breath, afraid now of the consequence of her little game. She was completely in his power. There was almost nothing he could not legally do to her. She heard the crack of the whip, and seconds later, felt him come alongside as he bent down to grasp the mare's bridle.

As the horse slowed to a stop he slid from the saddle and pulled Amy down with a savageness that made her cry out in pain.

"You stupid fool! Have you taken leave of your senses? What were you trying to prove?"

She was trembling so hard that she could not have answered even if she knew what to say. His grip on her was painful, yet she didn't want him to let go. He started to say something and then stopped midsentence as if sensing her desire. Grasping her by the wrist, he swore under his breath and dragged her half stumbling in the direction in which they were riding. Several times she fell but he lifted her up and continued to drag her along. When she thought she could bear no more he stopped abruptly and sunk his fingers into her mane of copper-colored hair.

"Look," he whispered through clenched teeth as he pointed downward with his free hand. "That's where you would be now if I hadn't stopped you in time."

Amy felt her face go white as she stared at the rocky ravine that stretched out below them. The path had ended abruptly but in her headlong flight she would not have known it until it would have been too late. The horror of her near brush with death came to her with vivid clarity and she wrenched her head free and stared at Jason with wide eyes.

"I . . . I might have been killed." The thought triggered something inside her and she felt an overpowering need to feel safe. Without thinking what she was doing, she threw her arms around him and rested her face against his chest.

Jason drew in his breath sharply as she felt his body grow rigid, and he looked stunned. Then, tangling his fingers in her hair, he tipped her head back and stared down at her as if seeing her for the first time.

The air was thick with emotion that closed out all thought but his nearness, and she felt her body sway toward him. With a groan he encircled her with his free arm and pulled her against him as his mouth found hers in bruising urgency.

There was surrender in her kiss and, at the same time, desire that bespoke only too well the passion that burned within her. Each movement, each tiny moan, only served to fan the flame of his compulsion until her lips were soft and swollen. But she welcomed the pain. She wanted it to last forever.

Without warning he thrust her away and turned his back toward her as he leaned against a tree. "My God, Amy. What have I done?"

Her eyes clouded at his sudden withdrawal. Her voice was high and tight. "What happened, Jason? Did I do something wrong?"

He bowed his head against his arm where it rested on the tree. "Forgive me, Amy. For a moment I forgot myself. I was so grateful to have you safe that I . . ."

She sank down on a bed of pine needles and patted the ground. "Sit down, please. There is no need to apologize. If anyone is to blame it is I for inviting the kiss."

"No. You were too young to know the consequences."

"Jason, please sit down."

He started toward her, then stopped midstride. "Get up and straighten your clothing. It's time we started back. The horses are badly in need of a rubdown and cooling off." He turned to fetch their mounts.

Amy got up slowly, feeling an emptiness that was more than hunger in the pit of her stomach. For the first time in her life she had wanted to give herself completely, and he had turned her away.

They rode back single file. All her attempts at conversation were either answered in monosyllables or were completely ignored. In the end she gave up the struggle and rode in silence.

There was no doubt in Amy's mind that Jason had been moved by their kiss. While it had lasted they had been touched with a passion that cast aside all their differences. His lips had burned a message more clearly than any spoken word could have done. As they approached the paddock she waited for him to ride alongside. His face was still set in rigid white lines, a clear sign that his anger was unabated.

She reached out and put her hand on his arm. "I'm sorry, Jason. It won't happen again."

"I should hope not." His voice was low and tight. "Suffice it to say that you leave yourself open to great injury when you entice a man by throwing your arms around his neck."

"But I—I wasn't talking about that. I meant that I would follow your rules about staying in the paddock until I have your permission to ride outside."

"It seems you have demonstrated your skill in the saddle. You have my permission to ride where you wish as long as you follow the trails. As for the other . . . had I realized you were given to such extremes of emotion, I would have been less tardy in finding a suitable husband for you."

"Are you trying to tell me that you want me to accept the marquis's proposal?"

"It has to be your own decision. That's the only way I'll have it."

"But I want to know what you think. Do you want me to marry him?"

Jason swore softly. "What must I do to get through to you?"

Amy pulled her horse to a halt and slipped from the saddle, looping the reins over the paddock gate. He got down to open the gate but stopped as she came close to him.

"Jason, I have to know what you want from me. Why won't you tell me what to do?"

"I can't, Amy. It's as simple as that."

"Is there some reason you think I should not marry him?"

"Not if that is what you want." He turned away as he spoke.

She studied him closely and saw the vein at the

base of his throat begin to throb in quick rhythm. "I don't believe you, Jason. I think you would like to marry me yourself."

His eyes opened wide and she found the courage to continue. "No man has ever kissed me the way you did, nor have I responded to any other man. I love you, Jason. I can't marry anyone else."

He started to reach out to her, whether in an embrace or in anger, Amy didn't know, but instead he opened the gate and mounted his horse.

"You talk like a child. Just because a man kisses you it does not follow that he is in love with you. It occurs to me that you are far too immature to know what you want. I shall inform the marquis that he must wait until my father returns for his answer."

Amy couldn't bear to look at him. Suddenly she was so tired that the least exertion required too much effort. "Would you please help me into the saddle?"

He sighed heavily but got down to assist her. When his arm brushed against her they both were embarrassed. Amy longed to touch his face, but this time the move had to come from him. Sweat beaded his forehead and he caught the inside of his cheek between his teeth as he looked at her. She waited, breathlessly, unable to keep the yearning from her eyes, but he tore his dark gaze away and bent down.

172

"Give me your foot and pull yourself into the saddle."

She obeyed without a word. In truth she hurt too much to talk. If he loved her as she had thought, there was some reason he had rejected her. Could it all have been her imagination? She had so little experience where men were concerned that she had no measure by which to judge. But he had wanted her, every instinct cried out it was so. Surely he was wise enough to know that he could have taken her there in the woods and she would have gone to him willingly.

The hurt was almost too much to bear. When they reached the stable she slid from the saddle and ran to her room without once looking back.

According to Polly who had been chatting with the local help, Lady Charlotte was again visiting with the squire and wasn't expected home until late.

"Great lackaday, Lady Amy. I've never seen 'er ladyship so smitten with anyone. Maybe hit's the country air. Blimey, they sure grow some 'ealthy lads 'ere at Winford Farms."

Amy looked up with surprise. "Are you telling me that you have found a young man so soon after having arrived?"

Polly flipped her skirts. "I'm not sayin' yes or no, miss, but that second gardener, name of Thomas Gately, is shapin' 'imself into right fine 'usband material. Mind you, though, I'm not sayin' I'll accept when he makes up 'is mind to offer for me."

But Amy could tell from the gleam in the girl's eyes that she would not hesitate long, given the chance to wed. Polly laid out the dressing gown and hung the riding costume in the armoire.

"Will there be anything else before you take your rest?"

"No, thank you. You may have some free time until teatime."

"Thank you, miss. I do fancy a stroll in the garden. Not that I'll be checking on Mr. Gately, but it does pay to know all about a man before settin' the trap."

Amy stretched out on the bed, a flicker of amusement lighting her face. Could it be that simple to get a man to propose? The way Polly saw it, all she had to do was decide on the victim and bait the trap. Would that it were so easy!

She reached her arm along the empty side of the bed and wondered how it would feel to have him lying next to her, to turn and see his head on the pillow, to feel his breath on her face. . . . With a strangled cry she jumped from the bed and began to pace the floor.

Her body ached with wanting him. Rest was out of the question. She needed something to occupy her mind. She started to reach for the bell-pull but remembered that Polly would be looking for Tom and decided to dress herself. She selected

174

a peach-and-white-striped cambric with a ruffle around the bottom of the skirt.

The sun baked the damp earth in the herb garden mingling the scents of rosemary, thyme, and mint, along with the other plants that formed the spokes of a wheel. She moved to the greenery where ferns and large-leafed foliage plants grew in profusion among the mossy crevices of an old stone wall. In the distance, beyond the topiary hedge, she saw the welcoming glimmer of the pond set in a clearing of willows and she turned her feet in that direction.

As she approached the tall yew hedge she heard voices coming from the other side and unconsciously slowed her footsteps. The voice was unmistakably Polly's.

"Now, Thomas, you watch your hands. I'm not a country servin' wench who gives you free rein to kiss and tumble as you please. I'm Lady Amy's personal maid and you best be rememberin'."

"Aye, lass. A lady's maid you might be but ye've no chance against me when I kiss ye." He chuckled low in his throat. "Blimey. Even Lady Amy Dorset 'erself wi' her foin 'ouse in Concordshire would take to a quick tumble after one o' my kisses."

Polly gasped aloud. "You just mind your tongue, Thomas Gately. If 'is Lordship 'eard you mention Lady Amy's 'ouse 'e would have you transported

175

to the Colonies. She's not to be told of 'er inheritance until she comes of age. Understand?"

He mumbled something unintelligible. Amy was so mystified that she stood still for several minutes, hardly daring to breathe. Inheritance? But surely the house in Concordshire had long ago been sold. Her father had moved to the town house in London after having vowed that he never wanted to see the ancestral home again.

Amy slowly retraced her steps to the house as she pondered the problem. But that was another thing. If her father had indeed sold the house, what had happened to all the money? He was not a gambler. He could not possibly have spent such a vast sum in those few years. She had never thought about it before, assuming that she was a veritable pauper from the way she had been forced to live at St. Catherine's.

But it made sense. Both Aunt Charlotte and Jason had acted most strangely whenever the subject of money or her expectations was brought up. And yet there always seemed to be enough to cover whatever expenses she might incur.

The footman looked up from polishing the silver as she passed him in the dining room and asked if Jason were at home.

"No, your ladyship." He bowed stiffly. "Lord Jason has asked to be excused from dinner. He has, I believe, plans to spend the night in Wal-

176

thamschurch. Her ladyship has just returned and is in her room if you wish to see her."

"Thank you, Harrison." As she slowly climbed the stairs to the second floor Amy tried to frame the question in her mind. She was certain the query would upset Aunt Charlotte but she had to know. Indeed it was her right to know where she stood financially. If she had a home of her own she wanted to see it. If she had money of her own it could mean the difference between marrying for money or marrying the man she loved. But no . . . Jason had little need for money. It would take something else to persuade him to offer for her.

Lady Charlotte looked surprised when she answered Amy's knock. "I thought you were resting. Marie said that you and Jason had spent the morning on horseback. What's wrong, dear? You look quite pale."

Amy sank down into a deep, soft chair without waiting to be asked. "Aunt Charlotte, you simply must tell me the truth."

Lady Charlotte sat down carefully on the edge of a straight-backed chair. "Of course, dear. What is it?"

"The mansion at Concordshire. Is it still in my family? Does it belong to me?"

Charlotte's mouth moved spasmodically but no sound came out. She moved the fan rapidly in front of her face as she forced a laugh. "My goodness. You young people ask the most pointed questions. In my day we would have approached the question of finances with a good deal more finesse. Why don't we have a pitcher of lemon water?"

"No, Aunt Charlotte. Not until you answer my question. I would ask Jason but he is away." She slid down onto the floor and took Lady Charlotte's fingers in her hand. "I'm going to find out, Aunt Charlotte, you can be assured of that. It is my right to know."

Lady Charlotte reached down and cupped Amy's face in her hands. "Yes, child, it *is* your right to know, even though your father did not agree. As much as I loved your father and always will, the man was hardly infallible. And in this . . . the way he treated you, he was surely wrong." She brushed Amy's hair back from her face. "It is Jason's place to tell you, but as you say, he has gone away unexpectedly and I can see that you are determined to know. Come, pull up a chair and I will tell you what I can."

CHAPTER ELEVEN

Amy slowly got up from her position on the floor and eased herself into a chair quietly lest she break Lady Charlotte's train of thought. She folded her hands expectantly as Charlotte tapped her fan against her hand.

"My, I wish Jason were here. It was so unlike him to dash off with hardly a by your leave." She sighed. "However, since you know this much you might as well know the rest." She eased a footstool into position with the toe of her slipper and leaned back. "It was your father's wish, as you know, that you be reared in seclusion until the time of your betrothal or such time as you came into your majority. Although he allowed for certain leeways he was adamant in one respect. That

179

was that you were not to be told of your inheritance until you came of age."

She shook her head. "It was foolish to imagine that we could keep the knowledge from you. Nearly everyone in the beau monde knows that you are an heiress, not to mention the servants. Indeed, the sevants are always the first to know the family secrets."

"But why was it so important that I not be told?"

Charlotte shrugged. "Your father was a strict disciplinarian. No doubt he felt that you might be tempted to join the theatre crowd as your mother had, or that you would be romanced by a no-good dasher who would squander away your money on games or women. The earl was far too proud of his heritage to allow that to happen."

"I—I remember the house. There were high stone walls . . . I had a room all of my own, with yellow curtains and yellow ruffles all around the bed. It looked out over the garden where there was a stone mermaid holding a pitcher which sprayed streams of water. I wonder what ever happened to it."

"I rather imagine it is much the same as it was then. After your mother left and you were sent away to school, your father closed the house and moved into the town house in London."

"But surely after all these years the house must be in a dreadful state of repair."

"I have no idea. As I recall he left a family in residence at the caretaker's cottage. I believe he also gave long-term rentals on the farmlands to the families who had worked the farms over the generations. It has been years since I was there but Jason would know."

"Have you actually been inside the house?"

"Yes, many times. I continued to be a friend of your father's even after he married." Her face turned crimson. "Please, don't misunderstand. Although I loved your father, I'm fairly certain that he never knew. I was also a friend to your mother and did my best to convince them to stay together."

Amy brushed it aside. "But then you know where it is."

"Concord House? Of course. It's at Concordshire, only a few miles east of here."

"Then I must go see it."

"I'm afraid that's not possible. Jason would never permit it without direct authority from the duke."

"But the duke may not return for weeks or even months!"

"Nevertheless you shall have to wait. We have already far exceeded the bounds of leniency provided for in your father's will. Really, Amy, you must consider Jason's position in this matter. Your behavior reflects upon him."

"You know I would never do anything to hurt him."

Lady Charlotte looked up quickly. "Strange. The way you said that I thought I detected . . . Amy dear, you haven't gone and fallen in love with my nephew, have you?"

Amy's face flamed, but before she could answer, Marie tapped at the door to Charlotte's sitting room.

"Beggin' your pardon, mum, but Lady Warrington has left her card and wonders if you are receiving guests."

Lady Charlotte made a face. "Oh, bother! Yes, tell Elizabeth that Lady Amy and I shall be pleased to see her. Then put her in the sun parlor and offer tea and cakes while we make ourselves decent."

Although Lady Elizabeth was the last person Amy wanted to see at the moment, she was grateful for the timely interruption. She could never have lied to Aunt Charlotte but her feelings for Jason were too precious to share. Rising quickly, she hurried to her room to change.

Lady Elizabeth rose to greet them when they entered the sun parlor together. Amy had to admit that Lady Elizabeth had never looked lovelier than she did at this moment, with the sun streaming through the window casting a golden halo all around her. She was like a vision in yellow, as she seemed to float across the white-and-moss-green Oriental carpet. Lady Charlotte took her hands and held them wide.

"Elizabeth, my dear, you look like a daffodil in the sun. Is this a new gown?"

"This old thing? Why, Lady Charlotte, you must have seen this a thousand times. I had it made at that little shop on St. James's Street. You know the one."

"Charmain Calvert's?"

"Yes." Lady Elizabeth turned to Amy. "And how sweet you look. Do sit beside me. We just haven't had a proper chance to chat."

Amy gritted her teeth. Small talk was something she detested. Fortunately Lady Charlotte was there to bear the brunt of the conversation and Amy was able to sit back and just listen. Her mind had begun to wander when Lady Elizabeth brought her back with a start.

"By the by, Lady Charlotte. Do you know where Jason has gone? He told me he would be away for a while, possibly several days."

"Oddly enough my nephew dashed off with hardly a word." She cocked an eyebrow. "I rather imagined he was with you."

Lady Elizabeth yanked her skirt around in irritation. "I'm sure he left a message to tell me where he would be but you know how servants are. . . ."

"Amy was having a riding lesson most of the morning. He left shortly after that, but he must have stopped at Mare's Run before leaving."

183

"Yes, just long enough to tell me he would not be having dinner with me. The poor dear, he looked exhausted. I had no idea the riding lessons would require so much time. It is so tiresome for him."

Lady Charlotte looked surprised. "I'm sure Jason doesn't find them so. In truth, he seemed to be looking more fit than he has for some time. The exercise is good for him."

"I only meant he needed a respite from his responsibilities. They have been overdemanding of late." She smiled quickly and changed the subject. "Charlotte, my dear, did you not say you would permit me to borrow the pattern you found for the green pelisse? My dressmaker is staying at Mare's Run for a few days and I thought she might have time to make up some gowns for my chaperon."

"Of course. I'll just run upstairs and fetch it." Amy rose to offer, but Charlotte waved her aside. "You would never find it, dear. I'll just be a moment."

Lady Elizabeth studied Amy over the rim of her teacup when they were alone. "Isn't she wonderful for an old woman? Charlotte has been like a mother to me. But I suppose that is to be expected. It is common knowledge that Jason and I are to be married."

Amy tried to control her voice. "Aunt Charlotte

doesn't seem old to me but I agree that she is wonderful. I care very much for her."

"As do we all. I hope she will help me plan my wedding. I have decided that it is time I give over to Jason, and we have set the date for a September wedding."

There was a terrible pounding in Amy's ears that could only be her own heartbeat. She wondered if Lady Elizabeth could hear it too. It was as if she had been shot, so great was the pain in her heart. She could not even gather the strength to reply but Lady Elizabeth seemed not to notice as she continued.

"But I don't suppose Jason has mentioned it. He is so terribly honorable about keeping his word and I swore him to secrecy." She giggled. "Now don't you tell a soul. I think of you as my little sister and I simply had to tell you."

Lady Charlotte returned at that moment with the pattern and put an end to the conversation. Amy hardly knew what else happened during Lady Elizabeth's visit. She was too stunned to let anything else penetrate her mind. Jason engaged! Impossible. How could he have held her and kissed her with such passion if he were in love with another woman?

After Lady Elizabeth took her leave Amy scurried off to her room with a feeble excuse and remained there until dinner. Food held no

185

temptation for her but she knew that if she refused to eat it would only arouse speculation.

Lady Charlotte interpreted Amy's mood as a result of the news of her inheritance and Amy made no move to enlighten her.

"Amy, dear, I know the news has come as a shock to you, albeit a pleasant one. I do suggest that you try to put it out of your mind for the present. As it stands your money will be kept in trust, save for whatever personal expenses you may incur. Any amount which exceeds your allowance would require previous approval by Jason."

Amy waved it aside. "The money doesn't concern me. I was thinking how my mother must have felt when she left us."

"It's no good dwelling on your past. Your mother was not a criminal, neither does she deserve to be put on a pedestal. We have enough to concern ourselves with with the future and finding you a suitable match. Tell me, have you thought more about your offer from the marquis? The time is fast approaching when you must make a decision."

Amy laid her spoon down carefully. "I—I discussed it this morning with Jason. I wanted his advice but he refused to give it to me."

"How perfectly odd. Just what did you tell him concerning your feelings on the matter?"

"I—I told him I am in love with someone else."

"Amy, you didn't! How could you make up such a preposterous story? You haven't known anyone long enough to fall in love." Amy said nothing but Lady Charlotte took one look at her stricken face and apparently realized something was amiss. She reached across the table for Amy's hand.

"Dear child, I'm afraid I have been dreadfully negligent in my duty as a chaperon. Please, let's go up to your room and you can tell me all about it."

When they were settled in the privacy of their sitting room, Amy drew herself into a corner. "I'm afraid there is nothing else to tell. I told Jason I was in love wi—with another man but I would do whatever Jason wanted me to do."

"Forgive me if I seem the nosey old woman, but as your chaperon, I feel I must take the liberty of asking the man's name."

"Please. I can't. I just can't."

"But perhaps I can help. If the man is suitable there is every chance that I can succeed in making the match. After all, with your youth, beauty, and expectations your potential is not to be taken lightly."

Amy jumped to her feet and went to stand by the window so that Charlotte could not see the agony written on her face. But her voice betrayed her emotion. "I'm afraid it's no use, Aunt Charlotte. The man's name is Jason."

"Jason! My Jason?" She hopped up and went

187

to stand behind her. "Forgive me, Amy. I didn't mean it to sound that way. Now that I think on it I am not surprised. Jason has a special appeal to women, but you couldn't have chosen a more difficult man to try to lure to the altar. He has often said that he has no time for marriage and will only take a wife when it is necessary for him to beget an heir." She put her arm around Amy's waist. "I wish there was something I could do to help you. Young love can be very painful."

"I'll just have to work it out for myself."

"Does Jason know?"

"Yes."

"Then that explains his sudden departure. He probably was unsure how to handle the situation without hurting your feelings."

"You make it sound like a childish crush. I love him, Aunt Charlotte, in the way a woman loves a man."

Lady Charlotte's face turned suddenly white. "Good heavens, he hasn't tried to . . ."

"No. But I wouldn't have stopped him."

Lady Charlotte let out her breath in a long sigh. "Well, under the circumstances, I perceive the need for a change in our living arrangements. When Jason returns I shall have to counsel with him on the advisability of our immediate return to London, assuming of course that it is *his* intention to remain here."

Tears stung Amy's eyes. "You want to keep

188

us apart, is that it? You think I'm not good enough to marry Jason."

"I have not even considered the possibility. Until I know Jason's thoughts on the matter I deem it foolish to conjecture." Her voice became gentle. "Surely you must realize I have a deep affection for you but there are many things to consider: your age for one, and Lady Elizabeth for another. You must know that she is expected to marry Jason. You cannot discount the hold she has on him."

Amy began to shake with unshed tears and Charlotte, sensing her distress, turned away. "I think you ought to get some rest. A pot of herbal tea would be the best thing for you right now."

As darkness fell Amy lay on the bed and listened for the sound of horses' hooves on the gravel drive leading to the stables, with the hope that Jason might decide to come home after all. The one bright spot was that he had chosen not to seek the comfort of Lady Elizabeth. But where had he gone? More frightening still, what would he say to her when he did return?

For the first time in years Amy wished desperately that she had a mother in whom to confide. It wasn't fair to ask Lady Charlotte to divide her loyalties. Where was her mother now? If she knew, she would surely go to her. But how could she find out where her mother was without asking questions? Questioning the staff would

189

only serve to alert Jason. No . . . there had to be another way.

It was nearing dawn when she found the solution. She would go to Concordshire, to her ancestral home. There perhaps she would find a clue as to where to begin her search.

At first she had planned to go on horseback, but since she was a stranger to the area, she thought it wise to have a driver who knew the countryside. Somehow she would work it out. Her confidence restored, sleep finally came.

Judging from Lady Charlotte's appearance at breakfast the next morning, she, too, had spent a restless night. In order to ward off questions Amy forced a bright smile and was pleased to hear Charlotte sigh with relief.

"I trust things look a bit brighter this morning. Perhaps Jason will be home today. He will know what to do."

Amy patted her hand. "I'm terribly sorry to cause so much trouble. You musn't let me spoil your day, Aunt Charlotte. As I recall you have been planning a game of whist with the squire for this morning."

"I shall send a message that I am indisposed. James will understand."

"Please don't. It would only serve to make me feel guilty."

"Well, if you are certain."

190

"Quite. I have a few chores I must attend to which will take most of the day."

While Charlotte dressed to go out Amy made plans of her own. She knew that it would take careful maneuvering to leave the house without her chaperon. Despite the fact that she was on good terms with the servants, she knew they typically enjoyed the least whisper of intrigue and would stop at nothing to explode the smallest incident into an event they could savor for weeks to to come. She could hardly go out alone and would have to trust someone. Polly was the logical choice. She was young enough to have a spirit of adventure and devoted enough to agree to her mistress's wishes.

As soon as Lady Charlotte left Amy pulled the bell rope to summon Polly. The girl looked puzzled when she saw the green linen traveling dress laid out on the bed.

" 'Ello, wot's this? Yer not plannin' to go out are you? 'Er ladyship has left without you."

"Yes, I know. But I must go out and I want you to go with me."

"Sure enough? An' where might we be goin' if I may ask?"

"I'll tell you about it later. But first I want you to go down to the stables and tell the groom that I want the small carriage made ready as soon as possible. Also tell him not to bring it to the front entrance. I will meet him at the stables."

"You want the groom and not the coachman?"

"Yes. I want a local boy who knows the country-side."

There was a hint of disbelief in Polly's voice. "Yes, miss, if you say so." She looked sly. "I'll wager 'e will want to know 'ow far we expects to drive."

Amy looked at her with exasperation. "Oh, very well. Tell him that we are going to Concordshire."

"Great lackaday!" Polly murmured, then saw the look on Amy's face and scurried out the door.

Amy's hands were shaking. She blew out her breath in a slow stream and leaned against the bedpost. She had taken the first step and now there was no turning back. Even if she changed her mind about going, Jason would still hear that she had considered going and that would be enough to infuriate him.

She had to go. It was her right to know about her past and what was left of it. For the first time in years she was going to see her home . . . the home of her ancestors. Concord House, whatever state it might be in, was her own, her very own. And soon, soon, she was going to see it.

CHAPTER TWELVE

The small carriage clattered through the edge of the village and into the open countryside but Amy saw little of the scenery. Her nerves were strung to the breaking point with the uncertainty of what lay ahead. The young groom had assured her that he could find the estate without any trouble, but even if they found it, would the buildings be in ruins after all these years?

When she saw Polly watching her with undisguised amusement Amy realized that she had been taking off and pulling on her gloves with endless repetition. She laced her fingers together in an effort to control herself.

"Did the groom say how long it would take to get there?"

"No, my lady, but I should wager less than two hours. Tim 'as a fair passion for movin' right along and 'e says the village is no more than twelve miles."

"Is it in Essex, then?"

"Yes, mum. If I'm not being too bold . . . just what is it you'll be expecting to do once we gets there? Will 'is lordship be there?"

"No, he won't. I just want to see my home. It has been twelve years since I last was there."

"Does 'is lordship know you are going there?" she asked in a sudden burst of boldness.

"I dare say he doesn't. But you needn't concern yourself. I fully intend to tell him all about it as soon as he returns."

Polly had the decency to look ashamed. "I wasn't about to spill it to 'im, Lady Amy. I'd 'ave my 'ead shaved first. I never did fancy keepin' the truth from you."

"It wasn't his fault. It was my father's decision."

There seemed to be nothing else to say and the women rode in silence for several miles. The countryside was dotted with small thatched-roof cottages, cows grazing in the pastures, children herding flocks of geese. Amy wondered how it could look so peaceful when her own world was in such turmoil. It was a bumpy ride partly from Tim's penchant for racing, but her eagerness to reach her destination precluded complaints about the slight discomfort.

By following the wooden signposts erected at each crossroad the driver was able to find the village without difficulty but was forced to stop at the blacksmith's and ask for directions to the estate. Within a few minutes he pulled himself up onto the seat and unhooked the reins as he leaned down to look through the window.

"Hit's not far now, your ladyship. We have only to drive to the yonder side of the village where the road splits three ways." He slapped the reins smartly and the carriage pulled ahead with a lurch.

Amy leaned forward expectantly. Nothing looked familiar but it would have changed in twelve years. Her first glimmer of recognition came when they crossed a narrow wooden bridge. In her mind's eye she seemed to see a group of children sailing their toy boats where the stream made a slow bend. The narrow lane that was rutted and fringed with bracken ended abruptly at a high stone arch with a heavy oaken gate. Tim tied off the reins and got down to open it but it was securely locked. He hesitated for a moment, then, seeing a bell which was partially concealed by vines, gave it a vigorous tug. It gave off a resonant, mellow sound which surely could be heard for miles.

After about five minutes a buxom woman with her hair tied in a thick plait at the back of her

195

head climbed the stile and peered over the top of the wall.

"I say, wot's the reason for all the racket? There be no one 'ere. The 'ouse is closed."

Not to be put aside, the groom drew himself up in a fine imitation of a gentleman and flourished his cap in a low bow. "Be so good, madame, as to open the gate. The Lady Amy Dorset's come to call on ye."

The woman bent low and shaded her eyes from the sun. "Be off with ye. Hit couldn't be 'er. 'Er ladyship is but a wee lass away at school."

Amy leaned her head out of the window. "Please do open the gates. I *am* Amy Dorset, daughter of the late Earl of Concord."

They could hear the woman catch her breath. "Glory be praised, miss, if you aren't the livin' image of your sainted mother." She disappeared and they could hear a heavy bar being drawn from its rack. Moments later the gate creaked slowly open.

When they arrived at the caretaker's cottage a few minutes later Amy learned that the caretaker was visiting one of the tenant farms, but the woman had all the keys to the mansion that lay just around a curve in the lane.

Her voice sounded wistful as she handed them over. "Be ye plannin' to open the house and live in it, your ladyship? All these years that's wot I've been prayin' for . . . that your mamma would come back." She wrapped her hands in her ample apron. "She's famous now, that one, but I knew she would be. She's a grand lady."

Amy was more than a little surprised to hear such praise for her mother, who was usually more maligned than lauded. "You knew my mother well?" she asked.

"Aye, that I did. Many's the time she sat at my kitchen table and talked about Mr. Shakespeare's plays. If I hadn't known you were her child I would have sworn she had come back to us. Of course she would be years older now and we haven't seen her for a long time . . . she's in Brighton, you know."

"In Brighton? Are you sure?"

"Aye, just a bit 'ere. She sent me a playbill from the Theatre Royal. I'll fetch it for you." The woman returned a minute later with a poster which she unfolded and smoothed with her hand. "There, ye see. 'Emily Concord plays the role of Portia in *The Merchant of Venice* by Mr. William Shakespeare.'"

Apparently seeing Amy's agitation at having seen her mother's name in print, the woman, whose name was Mrs. Harrington, put her hand on Amy's arm.

"Have you not seen her for a long time, child?"

Amy shook her head. "A very long time."

"Then 'ere. You keep this playbill. Mayhap you

197

will 'ave a chance to see 'er whilst she is in Brighton."

Amy folded it carefully and tucked it in her reticule. "Thank you. I shall treasure it. Now if I may have the keys . . . I'm most eager to see the house."

"Had I known ye was coming, my lady, I would 'ave red up the place but wi' nought to clean for it is right hard to keep it good."

Amy thanked her and told her they would return soon.

An instant after they rounded the bend in the lane the mansion sprang into view and with it the memories of childhood came flooding back. It was a cold looking house with straight lines unadorned by moldings, unsoftened by vines or shrubbery at the foundation. Long narrow leaded windows stared uncompromisingly from the gray stone exterior that was broken only by a large rotunda which served as a grand entrance or foyer. Tall pillars supported a huge overhang projecting over wide steps which led to a pair of massive doors. Amy remembered playing on those steps with her pet kitten, and remembered, too, the high pendentive arch that supported the dome of the entrance hall. She recalled lying on the cold slate floor as she watched the sunlight make a kaleidoscope of color in the rose, purple, gold, and blue stained glass windows that vaulted high above her. She remembered too the heavy wine-colored vel-

198

vet draperies in the library, where she had often secreted herself to avoid discovery while her parents had another of their many arguments. It was not a happy house . . . or could it have been the people who lived there that made it unhappy?

While the groom attended to the horse Polly accompanied Amy into the house. Surprisingly, instead of smelling stale and musty as she had expected, the air was scented with lavender blossoms and sweet-smelling rushes from the fields.

Polly caught her breath in admiration. "Great lackaday! The queen 'erself would be proud to own them stairsteps."

Amy followed her gaze to the twin staircases that rose like the wings of a swan to the second floor. On the wall between the stairs was an enormous tapestry which depicted the huntress Diana in a mythological woodland setting. Suspended in front of the tapestry was a majestic crystal chandelier which Amy remembered had been laden with branches of holly that shimmered beneath the candles on Christmas Eve. Her throat felt tight and she found it difficult to talk but Polly made up for it with a steady stream of chatter.

There were over thirty rooms in all, some of which were scantily furnished as befitted servants of the lowest rank. Most of the furniture was covered with white cotton dusters. Amy was surprised to find that everything seemed to be in fine condition considering that no one had been in residence for a period of years. Only the rear gardens that she could see from the upstairs windows appeared to have suffered from lack of care. The stable doors, too, looked closed and unused for a very long time.

She had saved her own room until one of the last. When Amy opened the door to her sun-yellow bedroom and adjoining playroom, it was as if she had stepped back in time to the days of her childhood. Save for the dusters on the furniture everything was just as she had left it the day she was sent to St. Catherine's. The carved white bed was shaped like a winged horse. Above it an oval canopy was draped with gauze to resemble clouds beneath which were suspended dozens of crystal stars that twinkled like diamonds in the moonlight. She moved to the toy room whose walls were lined with shelves which held miniature tea sets, stuffed toys, a collection of ivory elephants said to have been a gift from a dowager queen, and a bare place which had held Grimpy, her stuffed bear who had gone away with her.

Polly had been considerate enough to remain in the background but when Amy went to her mother's room, she felt an overpowering need to be alone. With a look of apology she asked her abigail to wait outside.

Polly nodded. "You'll be all right, miss? I'll wait downstairs if you need me."

Amy opened the door slowly and detected the

scent of rich, musky perfume, redolent of jasmine and expensive oils, that her father had purchased for her mother on one of his trips to India. If Amy had difficulty remembering her mother's face, the scent brought the image back with instant clarity. Her mother had used it on everything from bed linens to her own bath water until it had become as much a part of her as her own lilting laughter. The armoire was nearly empty save for a few outdated gowns and a mauve pelisse with a fur lining.

It seemed odd to Amy that her father had left the room intact. She would have thought he would be quick to dispose of anything that reminded him of his errant wife. But perhaps Aunt Charlotte was right. Maybe her father had never stopped loving his wife even after she had left him to become Emily Concord. She pressed the gowns against her face and breathed in her mother's fragrance. How different her life would have been if her mother had never run away. It would have been easier if her mother had died. Then, perhaps, Amy could have understood. She wanted so much to see her and touch her . . . and ask why.

How long she stood there Amy did not know, but suddenly she felt another presence in the room, and turned quickly. Jason stood in the doorway watching her, his hands above his head on each side of the doorframe, looking once more like the frightening bird of prey.

"Are you quite finished, Lady Amy?"

She felt her face go from flaming red to ashen gray. She did not speak but turned slowly away from him until she heard his footsteps behind her and his breath upon her hair as he waited for an answer.

"Why did you have to follow me, Jason? Couldn't you allow me these few hours alone with my memories of my mother?"

"Memories are like a disease. If you allow yourself to dwell on them they will eat you up inside. No good can come of your weeping over these old rags; that part of your life is over. You must plan for the future and let the past die a decent death."

She turned to face him at last. "Future, Jason? Just what do you have in mind? Marriage to a man whom you say wants me only for my ability to give him an heir? Or would you prefer to give me to someone who will squander my fortune on the horses or women after he tires of me? I wonder if my mother was not right after all. At least she took control of her life."

"You're talking like a fool. Come along. It's time we went home."

Amy laughed hysterically. "Home? I've never had a home."

"Your home is with me as you well know," he said, taking her by the shoulders. His face was so close that his breath stirred the fine hair at her

202

temples. The desire to throw her arms around him was so strong that she had to clench her hands against her side.

"I have no desire to make my home with you and Lady Elizabeth. I would rather die first." She whirled around and ran downstairs and out of the house. The startled groom was waiting with the horses. She climbed in and gave him orders to return to Winford Farms. Polly clambered aboard just seconds before he put the whip to the team. Amy glanced back once to see Jason turning the key in the lock of the main door. A few miles down the road he caught up with them and, signaling the groom to stop, tied his horse to the rear and climbed up on the seat next to the boy. Polly was bursting with questions but one look from Amy silenced her for the interminable ride home.

Lady Charlotte met them at the door, her face pale and drawn as she asked Amy if she were all right. Amy just looked at her and fled to her room. They left her alone until late in the day when Lady Charlotte came to sit beside her on the bed.

"What made you go there, child? Was it simply to see your childhood home?"

"I . . . I don't know. I think I wanted to feel closer to my mother."

"You had us very worried. Fortunately, Polly saw fit to tell the stableboy of your destination."

Amy knotted her fingers together. "I should

203

have never left Saint Catherine's. None of this ever would have happened."

"Don't talk like that. The picture will soon brighten. Fact of the matter is, I have some good news." A pink flush spread over her face as she pleated the edge of the bedspread. "The squire has again asked me to be his wife and I have agreed to marry him as soon as you are safely and happily married."

Amy threw her arms around her chaperon's shoulders. "Aunt Charlotte, I am so happy for you. You deserve a chance at happiness after all you have done for others. I hope you won't keep the squire waiting."

"Goodness. There isn't any rush. We have waited all these years, a few months more will not matter. Love is worth waiting for. Of course sometimes one waits in vain . . . as I did for your father, but I don't regret it for a moment. At the same time I have a great affection for the squire and will make him as happy as I possibly can."

Amy brushed her lips against Lady Charlotte's cheek. "The squire doesn't know his good luck in getting you."

Lady Charlotte stood up and smoothed her fichu into place. "The good fortune is mine . . . but come, you must dress for dinner."

"I really couldn't eat a thing."

"Nonsense. Jason will be furious if you don't come down."

"I can't see what possible difference it should make to him."

"Very well. But I cannot answer for the consequences should you fail to appear. Of late, Jason seems to be unusually short of temper, so unlike his old self."

Amy sighed. "I venture I'm to blame for that too."

Lady Charlotte scoffed. "Don't fret. A little upset now and then is good for everyone. I'm glad to see Jason react to someone. He was becoming too set in his ways, too sure of himself until you arrived. If truth be told I think he rather admires your courage in standing up to him . . . but I shall deny I ever said that, should you be so unwise as to quote me."

"I'm sure Jason would rather I had never been born."

Lady Charlotte patted her arm. "You are simply feeling melancholy. In a few days things will look brighter."

Amy thought about it after Lady Charlotte had gone. No, things would not look brighter unless there was a drastic change. And it was up to Amy to make that change soon because she couldn't go on this way. But the question was how?

Opening her reticule she took out the playbill

and smoothed it across her lap. It was difficult to realize that the words she read were about her mother. She remembered her mother's easy laughter and wondered, having been forced to give up the name of Dorset after her divorce, had her mother taken the name of Emily Concord, knowing full well that everyone would connect the name with the Earl of Concord? She carefully folded the poster and replaced it in her reticule, breathing a prayer of thanks that the caretaker's wife had seen fit to save it.

The thought of Mrs. Harrington reminded her of her quick exit from Concord House. She felt remiss in not having thanked the woman for her hospitality and she sat down to pen a quick letter which she would ask one of the servants to post. When it was finished she pulled a dress from the armoire without bothering to summon Polly. What did it matter how she looked?

She had just started buttoning the buttons on the front of her low bodice when there was a knock on the door. Thinking it was Polly, she picked up the letter and started to turn the key but Jason's voice interrupted her.

"Open the door, Amy. I want you to come down to dinner at once!"

She stepped back. "No, thank you. I prefer to stay in my room."

"Either you come out or I shall knock down

the door and fetch you myself," he said as he pounded on the door.

Amy recognized the venom in his voice. Out of sheer stubbornness she slipped through the sitting room to exit out the door of Lady Charlotte's room a few feet away. Jason, caught with his fist in midair, had the grace to look sheepish, but the expression soon changed. Puzzled, Amy looked down and realized too late that the soft swell of her breasts was revealed by the open buttons on her bodice. Her face turned scarlet as she attempted to cover herself. Jason stood stiffly aside as she swept past him on the way to the stairs.

She fumed silently. How could she have thought herself in love with this impossible man? He was stubborn and overbearing and he treated her like a child. Given enough provocation he would doubtless take her over his knees and spank her. She gritted her teeth. *Just let him try*, she thought. *Just let him try!*

By accident she had carried the letter with her. It was too large to tuck in her bodice but she laid it on her lap as Jason seated her at the table across from Lady Charlotte. She took a deep breath as she nodded to her chaperon. The air was thick with emotions too long suppressed. She had a feeling that tonight would mark the turning point in her relationship with Jason, and that knowledge was not the least bit comforting.

CHAPTER THIRTEEN

Lady Charlotte, seated at the table, was pale with concern as she looked at Amy. Their gaze, as it met for an instant, communicated their separate miseries, then Lady Charlotte nodded to the footman to begin serving. Amy unfolded her napkin, placing it over the letter that lay on her lap. Although the letter contained nothing of significance, being a simple thank-you note, Amy felt the less said about Concord House the better it would be.

The thought of food nearly turned her stomach but she made a pretense of eating the green herb soup with mushrooms. Lady Charlotte attempted several topics of conversation but neither Amy nor Jason contributed so much as a word. It soon occurred to Amy that Jason was watching her push the food around on her plate. He spoke suddenly and she was appalled at the harshness of his voice.

"It would appear, Aunt Charlotte, that we are rushing our dinner too quickly. Lady Amy has not had a chance to clear her plate."

Amy laid her fork down with finality. "On the contrary, Lord Jason, I have had enough. If I am hungry later I shall send to the kitchen for something to eat."

"You'll dine with us or you'll go hungry."

"Children, children," Lady Charlotte interjected. "Enough of this nonsense. I forbid you to quarrel. What has happened to the two of you that you show such utter disregard for each other's feelings? Can't you see how upsetting it is?"

Amy bit her lip. "I'm dreadfully sorry, Aunt Charlotte. It was not my intention to distress you." She picked up her napkin and brushed her lips to conceal the quiver of her chin. As she did so the envelope on her lap went flying halfway across the room and a footman went to pick it up. He started to hand it to Amy but Jason intercepted it with a quick movement of his hand.

"I'll take that, if you please." He turned it over and looked at the address and then at Amy. "Why should you find it necessary to write to the housekeeper at Concord House, and why should you be so secretive about it?"

Amy felt the heat rise in her face. "I have no wish to discuss it. The letter does not concern you."

"Indeed?" His tone was dry. "Everything you do concerns me, Lady Amy."

"Then I'm sure we will both be relieved when I put an end to your responsibilities. My only regret is that that end seems nowhere in sight. For the present I would appreciate the return of my letter so that I may give it to a servant for posting."

He tapped the envelope against the rim of his wineglass. "Would you be so good as to tell me the contents of the letter?"

"I see no reason to do that."

"Then I shall read it for myself."

Lady Charlotte's hands flew to her face. "Oh, Jason. You mustn't! You're treating her like a child. Can't you see she's a grown woman?"

His face turned scarlet and to Amy's indignation he picked up a silver knife and slid it between the envelope and the dab of pink sealing wax. Without looking at either of them he took the letter out and read it, then folded it and slipped it back into the envelope as he cleared his throat.

"Very well. I see no reason it may not be sent. I will ask the footman to post it."

Amy had to fight to keep back her tears. "That will not be necessary," she said as she held out her hand for the letter. When Jason gave it to her she looked him full in the face and slowly, deliberately, tore it into pieces, bit by bit. Still holding him with her gaze, she held her hand above her head and let the pieces fall in a silent blizzard all over the table in front of her.

Jason swore softly and for a moment Amy thought he would come at her in anger but he remained in his chair. With that Amy got up and walked to the doorway, pausing at the last minute to drop a curtsy to Lady Charlotte and asking to be excused. She felt a small glimmer of triumph in the knowledge that Jason was too stunned to rise . . . not to mention protest.

Amy went directly to her room, locked both doors, and settled in for the night. In truth she was too exhausted both mentally and physically for anything else. Sleep was a long time coming and she rose several times to walk to the window to breathe the fresh air. There was another reason. She found great satisfaction in knowing that the light in Jason's study remained on long after his usual time to retire.

As she lay there courting sleep she remembered what Lady Charlotte had said about Jason. Beneath his grim exterior Amy had detected a flicker of admiration, if not outright amusement. She curled her fingers around the corner of her pillow, a holdover from childhood habits. The image of his face so near to hers floated before her eyes and she forgot how angry she had been as she smiled at the ludicrousness of life. It took such a small weight to tip the balance of scale between hatred and love.

When she opened the door to Polly the next morning, her abigail looked miffed at having been locked out. She gave Amy an "I told you so" look and sailed past without so much as a good-morning. When Amy took a plain cotton frock from the armoire Polly looked disdainful.

"I thought mayhap you would be wanting something a little more becoming, your ladyship." Her voice held a hint of slyness. "'Is Lordship 'as been waiting for you in the study for over an hour."

Amy sighed. "And what would you suggest?"

"Judging from 'is look, miss, I would pick the tightest, most low-cut gown I could find."

"He's that angry?"

"Not exactly, but I'll wager 'e spent a sleepless night. 'Er ladyship is with 'im."

Amy sobered. Either one alone she could handle but the two of them at this time of day meant they had been discussing her. Prudence told her it was better not to delay.

Jason met her at the door and ushered her to a chair, then seated himself behind the desk. Amy took a deep breath and decided to meet them head-on.

"I'm sorry if I have kept you waiting. I was

not aware until moments ago that you wished to see me."

Lady Charlotte waved her fan in a nervous flutter. "No need to apologize, Amy."

Jason looked haggard and Amy felt a twinge of conscience at having been the cause of his discomfort. He yanked irritably at his waistcoat as he pushed out his lower lip in a pensive gesture. Amy flushed as she remembered how warm and sweet his mouth had felt against hers, and it was with considerable difficulty that she concentrated on what he was saying.

"I am forced to agree with Aunt Charlotte. I think it is most important that the two of you return to London on the morrow and remain in seclusion until the duke returns. I expect him to arrive within two months at the most. In the meantime, I shall remain here at Winford Farms."

Amy's chin began to tremble. "Why are you doing this to me, Jason? Why couldn't you have left me at Saint Catherine's?"

His mouth was a thin white line and his knuckles, where he laced his hands together, stood out starkly against his brown hands. Lady Charlotte spoke in a gentle voice.

"My dear, we only want to protect you and raise you the way your father would have wanted."

"But my father saw my mother in me . . . the part of her that deserted him. I am not my

213

mother, neither am I a child to be punished and kept in seclusion."

Lady Charlotte reached for her hand. "And that is it, isn't it? You are not a child, but a lovely, innocent woman who has suddenly awakened to find herself a wealthy and desirable heiress. You still have a great deal to learn about the responsibilities of wealth."

"And what I want has nothing to do with it?"

"It is to be hoped that we both want the same thing."

Amy turned toward Jason. "It's settled then?"

He nodded without speaking. There was a long pause, during which he turned to stare out the window.

Amy knotted her fingers in her handkerchief. "And what about Aunt Charlotte? Must she wait all that time to marry the squire? It seems uncommonly cruel to deprive her of happiness simply to provide me with a keeper."

Jason whirled around. "It isn't like that at all and you jolly well know it. We just feel that you ought to mature a bit before being forced to make important decisions concerning your future. Think calmly about it and you will agree."

"You are wrong, Jason. Fact of the matter is . . . I have already made a decision. I have decided to accept the most generous offer of marriage from the Marquis of Melmoth." Even Amy herself was shocked by her words but Jason was

214

outraged. His face went white as he stood, gripping the edge of the desk.

"You must be totally mad! How could you say such a thing?"

Lady Charlotte's voice shook uncontrollably. "I—I really think you should curb your tongue, Amy. You have made it abundantly clear that marriage to the marquis would be only a convenience." She rose. "I think it wise if we put an end to the discussion for now. In a few weeks after we have returned to London, we will have things more in focus. Now if you'll excuse me I have packing to do and I shall require a few hours this afternoon to make my explanations to the squire."

Amy rose to follow her but Jason stopped her with a look. He strode over and closed the door behind Lady Charlotte who first gave him a look of warning. Then he came over to where Amy stood and took her by the shoulders.

"All right. You have made your point. There is no need to dramatize this into a full-scale war. You have had your little joke, but if you think I have altered my decision, you are badly mistaken."

Amy's voice came low and deadly from deep inside her. "I was not jesting, Jason. I spoke in all sincerity. As soon as the arrangements can be made I plan to become Marchioness of Melmoth."

"I'm afraid you will find it too late for that. I have already sent word to the marquis that you extend your appreciation and your regrets."

215

She smiled coldly. "Somehow I don't think he will mind if I tell him I have had a change of heart and desire to become his wife. He, at least, finds me attractive."

Jason swore competently. "You go too far, Amy."

"But not far enough to be out of your sight. Isn't that what you really want, Jason . . . to get me out of your sight until I am no longer a responsibility? You don't need my money, and you obviously want me nowhere near you. The marquis at least enjoys my company. If truth be told I suspect he will be a fairly competent lover. His kisses, at least, show a marked degree of expertise."

His face was livid with rage. "You—you permitted him to touch you?"

"Isn't that what one does when one is in the company of the opposite sex? I daresay you have sampled your share of lips without surrendering your precious freedom. As I recall you condescended to kiss me on more than one occasion."

She walked toward the door. "But have no fear. I shall allow you to save face by permitting you to tell the marquis that I am willing whenever he is ready to make me his bride." She held up her hand to still his retort. "But if you refuse, I shall go to him, wedding or not."

He lunged after her, slamming her against the door, and held her there with the weight of his body. With his free hand he wrenched her chin upward and ground his mouth against hers. His kiss was of anger, lacking even the slightest degree of warmth. He wanted to hurt her and this, just short of violence, was the only way he knew how. She understood and refused to struggle. Despite herself she felt the blood race along her spine and he drew back, a look of triumph on his face.

"Now tell me you want to marry the marquis."

Amy felt her face go scarlet. How she hated him at that moment. Her voice became low and seductive. "Don't worry, Jason. After a few hours in the arms of my husband, I'm sure it will be hard even to remember your face."

Reaching up with her hands on each side of his head, she pulled his face down to hers. With infinite care she kissed him full on the mouth, softly at first, but with ever-increasing movement until she felt the blood sing in her ears. As the kiss held she insinuated herself against him, knowing full well that he could define every curve and hollow in her body. Then, as quickly as it began, she thrust him away from her and opened the door, only to look back with a parting shot.

"Remember that come September when you lie in your marriage bed with Lady Elizabeth." She waited just long enough to see the look of shock on his face. So . . . he didn't know that she knew about the engagement. Well . . . if she had broken Lady Elizabeth's trust it was just one more sin for which she would have to answer.

She ran up the stairs and bolted the door behind her. A short time later she heard a carriage spew gravel as it slued around the semicircular drive. It was only Jason's skill as a horseman that saved the phaeton from turning over as the team put their teeth to the bit and lunged forward.

Amy turned away from the window with an aching heart. She felt more alone now than when her father had left her at St. Catherine's. But she was no longer five years old, and there were no tears left. Her father was dead and she had, for all practical purposes, no mother. She lived in a house of strangers who made the rules and would continue to do so until she took charge.

As if in a dream she went to the chest and took the playbill from her reticule, unfolding it on top of the desk. She knew what she had to do. It was as if she had always known. She would find her mother. But it would not be easy. She would have to plan each detail as if preparing for war. Indeed, there would be a battle royal if either Aunt Charlotte or Jason were to find out before the plan was accomplished.

As much as she trusted Polly it was clear from her last experience that Polly's first loyalty was to Jason. Amy knew that she had to do this alone. Therefore she would be unable to use the carriage. It would have been too scandalous for her to even think the stableboy would send a carriage for her without benefit of chaperon. No, her only hope was to go on horseback. Jason had said she could have the freedom of the estate, and they would not be surprised if she wanted a last ride before they departed for London in the morning.

She mentally added the miles and remembered with dismay that Brighton was about seven hours by coach. Too far, much too far to attempt on horseback . . . but she could leave the horse at the stable in Milsham and continue on by coach that stopped at the coaching inn to pick up and discharge passengers.

The very thought gave her cold chills. She had never ridden on a commercial coach and had no idea how much it would cost. She ran to the chest and removed a bag of coins which she had saved from her quite generous allowance. The amount was rather substantial. Indeed it would be enough to keep her quite modestly until she found work of some sort to help pay her way. The only problem was how to leave the house with enough clothing to last but not enough to arouse suspicion. There would be personal necessities too.

She began to pace the floor. A valise would be far too obvious. She could wear an extra gown beneath her riding costume but that would hardly begin to fill her needs. A picnic basket! It was the perfect solution. No one would take a second look if she went riding with a picnic basket slung over her arm. It was one of the favorite pastimes of the people in the country villages.

She had yet to eat breakfast. Only heaven knew when she would eat her next meal. It would be better, too, not to give the staff more cause to speculate about her. She hurried down to the kitchen and asked for a pot of tea and a plate of toast. While it was being prepared she asked cook to prepare a picnic lunch for her to take in the picnic hamper when she went riding to the deer park.

After she had eaten she went up to her room to dress in her riding costume of a soft tan with a dark brown cape. Its ample hood would adequately conceal her hair which she pulled back into a tight coil behind her head.

A few minutes later she heard the door to Lady Charlotte's room close and watched out the front window until she was sure her chaperon had left for the squire's house in the carriage. Polly tapped at the door and came in about then.

"Cook said you were going riding. I came up to 'elp you dress and if you won't be needin' me for a while I'd like to take the time to say my goodbyes to Thomas Gately. I brought the picnic hamper cook packed for you," she said as she placed it on a low stool.

Amy was grateful for the ready-made excuse to get Polly out of the room. "I know how hard it will be for you to leave now and go back to

London. I can manage getting dressed. You go out to the garden and spend as much time as you can with Thomas. I'll send for you when I need you."

Polly raised an eyebrow but was not about to question her good luck. Amy continued. "Please ask the groom to saddle my horse when you go out. Jason has given me permission to ride alone and I plan to spend the day in the deer park."

Polly dropped a curtsy and disappeared with a flash of skirts.

It had all been too easy. Amy felt in her bones that something had to go wrong. Jason kept such a close watch over her all the time. She had never been able to stay out of his sight for very long. She shrugged. All she could do was take each move as it came. She quickly folded the clothing she had selected, dumped the contents of the picnic hamper in the back of the armoire, and packed her personal things in the basket. She had taken an extra cloak in a small valise but decided it was too obvious and left it in the armoire. As she hung her discarded gown in the armoire and smoothed her riding skirt down over her hips, she looked around the room.

Suddenly the enormity of what she was doing hit her like a blow. She was leaving everything she loved behind her . . . and for what? A mother who might not even admit to knowing her, a future with no guarantee of security. It would be many months before she could claim her inheritance without interference from Jason.

Was she being foolish? No! She had no other choice. She couldn't bear the thought of going to London without Jason. Better by far to cast him out of her life while there was still time. She brushed away a tear from the corner of her eye. *Admit it,* she thought. *It's not the house you hate to leave, it's Jason.* He would be returning soon. If she was going to leave it had better be now. Pulling the cape around her shoulders, she picked up the picnic basket and closed the door behind her with hardly a backward glance.

CHAPTER FOURTEEN

An hour later Amy sat in the main room of the coaching inn waiting for the stage to arrive from London on its way to Brighton. Her arrival had attracted no small amount of attention as might be expected for a young girl traveling alone. The stablemaster in particular looked at her with curiosity as she attempted to make arrangements to have her horse delivered to Winford Farms the following day.

The figure he quoted for the service seemed astronomical, and although she had enough money, she decided to protect her investment by paying half of the fee, with the remainder to be paid upon delivery. She drafted a hasty note of explanation to be given to the steward at the farm.

Now, sitting beneath the low, heavy looking rafters in the daub-and-wattled room, she smiled at her own ingenuity. Not only had she made certain the horse would be cared for, she indirectly provided the information that she was reasonably safe. It had seemed wise not to leave a note informing them of her destination. Jason, with his penchant for chasing after her whenever she strayed, would find out soon enough where she had gone.

The inn fairly bulged with travelers. Even now a group were being loaded onto the mail coach to take them to the inn at Dover. Her own coach was due to arrive in less than an hour. She had to hide a smile as she saw the way passengers and freight were packed into every available inch of space. In addition to the fourteen passengers, there were trunks, valises, portmanteaus, mail sacks, and wooden boxes which were loaded on top or lashed to the sides.

Amy felt a surge of pity for the four horses as they pawed at the ground and rolled their eyes, snorting with impatience. The only comforting thought was that the stage owners saw to it that fresh horses were available at every stop, not so much for the comfort of the horses, but in the interest of speed.

The noise diminished somewhat after the coach departed, but the considerable hubbub from the adjoining gaming room continued to draw her gaze. One man sporting a thin mustache had been watching her for some time and she tried to avoid meeting his eyes. Two older people dozed against the wall in the corner, and a plump middle-aged woman sat at a table near the far wall, while her three children quietly shared a bag of tarts.

Amy had been so intent on watching the children she was unaware that the man had risen until he sat down very close to her, his breeches and coat brushing her hip.

"My compliments, miss, or is it madam? It distresses me to see a lady travel alone among the rabble and it behooves me to offer my services as a protector until we reach Brighton." He smiled confidently. "Yes, I took the trouble to inquire of your destination at the ticket purveyor's booth."

"Thank you, but I assure you I can manage quite well." As his arm slid across the back of the bench Amy looked around in desperation. She dared not create a scene for fear of calling attention to herself but she felt defiled by his presence. She pulled her cape more closely around her. "My husband will be here shortly. Until then I prefer to sit alone."

He threw his head back and laughed. "Husband indeed! I doubt that you have seen seventeen summers, let alone tasted the fruits of the marriage bed."

Amy moved along the bench but he slid along the seat after her. She could smell the sickening

225

odor of secondhand ale on his breath as he put his arm across her shoulders. At that moment Amy saw the plump woman whisper something to the three children who immediately got up and came over to where Amy and the man were sitting. The youngest reached up her hands to Amy who lifted the child on her lap, while the older children arranged themselves close to her.

The man drew back in surprise. "Are these all your children?"

Amy assumed a haughty expression. "Hardly! The two youngest are at home with their grandmother. Surely you don't think I would be so insensitive to take them on such an arduous trip?"

He murmured something unintelligible and departed. With a grin to match her ample bulk, the children's mother heaved herself from the chair and came to sit beside Amy.

"Aye, there's nought to dampen a man's amorous intentions like a passel of children. I'm hoping I guessed right, miss. 'E looked like 'e was up to no good."

"I can't thank you and your dear children enough. I—I really didn't know what to do."

The woman lifted the squirming child from Amy's lap. "Twas a pleasure to see 'im put in his place. But tell me, miss, are you all right?" She looked faintly embarrassed. "Wot I mean is, 'tis a bit out of ordinary to see a young lady of quality traveling alone." Apparently seeing Amy's look of surprise, she smiled. "Aye, you didn't think you could 'ide it, did you? Those boots alone cost more than my 'Enry makes in a month."

"I'm sorry . . . I—"

"Oh, now . . . I didn't mean to shame you." She looked speculative. "I'll wager that you've run away from 'ome."

Amy blushed. "You are partly right. I'm going to Brighton to visit my mother. She is an actress at the Theatre Royal."

"But of course. I knew you looked familiar. Your mother must be Emily Concord. I've seen 'er passin' on the street and saw 'er picture on a playbill. They say she is as talented as she is beautiful."

They continued to talk about Brighton, which proved to be the woman's home, and about the beaches and the Royal Pavilion where the Prince Regent often lived in lavish splendor. When the coach finally arrived they managed to sit together during the long ride to Brighton. Mrs. Wheatly gave Amy careful directions to the theatre and told her that she would help her find transportation once they arrived at their destination.

Once there, she held true to her word by seeing Amy aboard a cabriolet after having given the driver explicit instructions to see Amy safely to the theatre. It was with a genuine sense of loss that Amy said good-bye to the friendly woman and her three children.

As the small carriage rumbled through the cobbled streets Amy searched her reticule for the playbill, wanting once again to reassure herself. When she was unable to find it she nearly panicked but remembered she had put it in the small valise she had left behind. What did it matter? She had memorized every word. In no time the driver dropped her in front of the Wright's Royal Colonnade Library which he said was as close as he could get to the theatre, it being time for the matinee to let out. She paid him and thanked him for his service, then collected her picnic basket and climbed down, with more than a slight shaking to her legs. Now that she was here she began to wonder if she had made the right decision.

The theatre proved to be just around the corner. It was a fairly simple building with a portico and a colonnade of square columns which continued on around the corner to the library that was also a music saloon and reading room. Amy surveyed the two-story building whose front drive was crowded with fashionable carriages waiting to receive their noble passengers. She was less than eager to face that crowd. Instead, she continued on around to the mews behind the theatre until she found the stage entrance, and went inside.

It took a few minutes for her eyes to become accustomed to the dimly lit corridor. She could hear softly muted voices coming from the far end and moved toward them with the hope that someone would be able to direct her to her mother's dressing room. As she approached the conversation stopped midsentence and as they all turned to stare at her, Amy heard someone gasp aloud. A well-dressed man separated himself from the group and came toward her, both hands extended in greeting.

"What a smashing surprise. It do believe it is Lady Dorset, is it not? The last time I saw you, you were being dragged unceremoniously away from your performance at Penridge Castle. Or have you forgotten how you baptized those poor cocks in lemon water?"

Amy tried to pull her hands away without appearing prudish. "I haven't forgotten. Count Borelli, isn't it?"

He bowed low. "I'm flattered, my lady. Tell me, what brings you to Brighton? Your mother told me nothing of your impending visit."

"She was not expecting me. I . . . I came on impulse. Would you perhaps know where I might find her?"

His eyes glinted. "Indeed, I always know where to find her." He smiled suggestively. "If you will be very quiet you may watch from backstage while she performs Scene Four, Act One of the *The Merchant of Venice*." He took her hand and led her through a tall door to an area near the entrance to the stage.

229

Amy was afraid that the entire building could hear the beating of her heart. She was both excited and anxious about seeing her mother for the first time in many years. A quick glimpse of the packed house was enough to convince her of her mother's popularity among theatregoers. The audience listened as if they were a single being intent on hearing each word, each nuance of speech that ushered from Emily Concord's mouth. Amy caught her breath. Her mother, looking even more beautiful than she had remembered, stood in the robes of a barrister with her hand resting lightly on a railing at center stage. Her voice was rich and vibrant with emotion as she spoke Mr. Shakespeare's immortal words.

"The quality of mercy is not strained,
It droppeth as the gentle rain from heaven
Upon the place beneath. It is twice blessed—"

Amy listened entranced as she forgot that the woman on stage was not Portia pleading in the court of justice in her defense of Antonio, but, indeed, her own mother. It was only when the play had finished and her mother and the other players made their final bows that Amy returned to the reality of the present.

Count Borelli put his hand on Amy's waist and led her onto the stage that was now curtained from the view of the audience. Emily Concord,

230

the glow of triumph shining like an aura around her, turned as they approached. Amy saw the color drain from her mother's face as she reached for the back of a chair for support. Count Borelli spoke.

"Emily, my dear. Look who I've brought you," he said, gloating over the sensation they were causing.

Her mother's voice was scarcely a whisper compared to the resonancy she had exhibited on stage. "Amy, child, is that really you or are you a ghost of my own youth come back to haunt me?"

Amy fought back the tears. "Mother . . . I've waited so long for this day." She reached out her arms and they enfolded each other in a warm embrace. Gone were all the doubts about her mother's love for her; forgotten, all the hurt and desolation she had known after her mother had gone away. It was true, her mother loved her and that was all that mattered.

To escape the curious who crowded around them, they went to the dressing room where her mother changed into a bright red muslin trimmed with rows of yellow silk flowers at the neck and hemline. Amy felt that it was quite gaudy considering her mother's mass of bronze hair, but she assumed that stage people dressed rather differently. They had little time to talk then and even later on the way to the Old Ships Inn where the players made their temporary homes. It seemed everyone who could piled into the carriage with them, eager to hear the details of the unexpected happening.

"Is she really your daughter, Emily? You never told us you were a mother," one pretty young girl declared.

A bearded man spoke up. "She is so ravishing, my dear, that she could only be the daughter of Emily Concord."

The young girl smirked. "Aye, but I wouldn't want a daughter around me who looked like that. It would make people begin to wonder about my age."

Emily Concord tensed visibly, then waved a hand in disdain. "Don't be silly, Daisy. Amy is still a child, as I was but a child when she was born. Why, she is still in school! So you see . . . your worries are without foundation."

Count Borelli laughed. "Child she may be, but when I saw her performance of Katharine in *The Taming of the Shrew* at Penridge Castle, she looked more the wanton woman than the wayward child."

All faces turned toward Amy but none evidenced more surprise than Amy's mother.

"Amy, don't tell me you, too, have an affection for the stage?" Her mother was aghast.

"No. I—"

But Count Borelli refused to let her finish.

232

"Affection or not, she has a talent similar to yours, Emily. With a little training I'll wager she could give you some serious competition."

Amy looked at her mother's face and for the first time saw the ravages of age, the network of fine lines that had been concealed by the heavy paste and wax makeup used on stage. She sensed her mother's discomfort and attempted to change the subject.

"Judging from the applause at the end of the play it would seem to me that none of you need be concerned for your careers. Are the audiences always as well dressed?"

The bearded man nodded. "Brighton's Theatre Royal caters to the cream of the nobility. Partly, I suppose, because the Prince Regent is frequently in residence at the Royal Pavilion. Then, too, the town is a favorite holiday retreat for those who enjoy the bathing machines or a stroll along the shore or a leisurely walk along the Stiene."

Count Borelli agreed. "The fashionable clientele contribute to the metropolitan flavor of Brighton." He laughed. "Although you may not find them staying at the Old Ships Inn as we do, preferring instead the fashionable Castle Inn, you will discover that we have a more enjoyable time."

Emily smiled. "That is most considerate of you, Count, since we are aware that you could easily afford the Castle Inn." She turned to Amy. "Some of the world's greatest have performed here, child. Mrs. Siddons, whom they call the Queen of Tragedy, Madame Vestris, Joseph Grimaldi, William Macready, Edmund and Charles Kean, and dozens of others. Some of us began at the old Duke Street Theatre but a kindly providence has seen fit to take us to the top."

A silence followed her words as if those in the company had relived in an instant the desperate years of struggle and frustration.

Amy was moved by their introspection and knew she should have kept silent but was forced to inquire, "I can understand your triumph at having reached the pinnacle, but how can you survive, knowing that fame is, at best, fleeting?"

They looked at her with pity and several people made comments but the bearded man summed it up for them all. "I doubt that an outsider could comprehend how we feel about the art. The only failure, my dear, is in never having tried."

"Hear, hear . . ." The cheers went up and Amy was surprised to see moisture glistening in their eyes.

Her mother's room at the hotel was small and dingy, nothing at all like Amy had anticipated it would be. Clothing was strewn about in untidy heaps as if her mother had selected then discarded a number of different gowns until she finally chose the one which fitted her mood.

They were alone at last . . . but only temporarily. The members of the cast were like a family and they wanted to share Amy as if she were one of their own. Traveling around as they did, the players had little chance to be with their families, if indeed there were any among them who still had families to call their own. Before leaving her they extracted a promise that she and her mother would dine with them before the next performance.

Emily Concord swept the clothing off a chair onto the floor and collapsed into it. "Do sit down, Amy, and tell me all about this. You say you are no longer in school? It was my understanding that the Duke of Haddonfield had been appointed your guardian. I cannot believe that he would have permitted you to come here unescorted."

Amy pleated the edge of her riding skirt. "What I said was true . . . Mother." She hesitated over the word. "I really did run away, though not from school. Lord Jason Winford, the duke's son, is acting as my guardian until the duke returns. It was he who decided nothing was to be gained by keeping me in school, and it was from his authority I fled."

"You hate him that much?"

"Hate him? Oh, no. I could never hate Jason! At least not for very long."

Her mother smiled knowingly. "Ahh. Then you are in love with him. No . . . don't bother to deny it. It is written all over your face. You never

235

could lie to me, Amy, although you rarely tried. You were a good child and you deserved better than I had to offer." She looked down for a moment and was silent, then took a deep breath and looked up. "But how is it that you came unchaperoned?"

"Aunt Charlotte was not aware of my intentions or she would never have permitted me to come to Brighton."

"Charlotte? Lady Charlotte Winford, the duke's sister?" Emily chuckled. "Ah, yes, indeed. She couldn't succeed in getting my husband but she managed to get my child." When Amy began to protest her mother waved her aside. "Forgive me. I did not mean to sound peevish but I find the situation amusing. Lady Charlotte could easily have been your mother instead of me. Heaven knows she wanted the job badly enough but she was always too much the lady to fight for her cause. I doubt that your father ever knew she was in love with him."

Amy didn't know what to say and sat there, enduring her mother's speculation. "You've turned into a beautiful young woman. More beautiful than even I was at your age." The way she said it could not be construed as conceit, but merely a statement of fact. "And what are your plans now, my dear? Will you be able to stay in Brighton a day or two so that we may have a chance to get to know one another?"

"I confess I have no immediate plans. I thought perhaps you might—"

Her mother cut in before she could finish "I'm sure you realize it would be impossible for you to stay here, much as I would adore having you with me. The people here are . . . well, you met them. They are not your sort, Amy. Your education and breeding have put you in another class. They would destroy you in a month's time. You obviously know Count Borelli. You know what he is like. He takes everything and gives nothing in return, except an occasional brief moment of pleasure." She leaned back and tilted her head to stare at the ceiling. "We are all like that in the theatre. We have to put ourselves first. It is the survivor instinct, I suppose. If we don't take care of ourselves, no one will do it for us. The count has other reasons than survival, but he has followed us for so long that he has become like one of us."

Amy had gotten the message. There was no place for her here. And yet, strangely, she didn't love her mother any the less for her attitude, nor did she feel any bitterness toward her. Rather, it was an acceptance of things the way they were. Aunt Charlotte had told her that some people had a destiny of their own to follow and could permit nothing to stand in their way. What good to fret over things when there was no hope in changing them? Better to continue on and make the best of it.

237

Emily Concord stirred in her chair. "You look pensive, Amy. I hope I have not completely unsettled you. I want you to have your chance at happiness as I have had mine."

"Are you then truly happy, Mother?"

She smiled. "You're wondering how I can be amidst all this." She motioned with her hand, taking in the general disorder of the room. "I know. Compared to Haddonfield Hall and the other palatial houses owned by the duke, this must look like the very dregs. And I admit it. Now and then I have a certain longing for the feeling of luxury around me, particularly when I'm shivering from the cold in my cotton cloak. But when I walk out there on the stage and hear the applause begin at the front of the audience and roll backward like some great tidal wave, I know the realization, the culmination of all I have worked and sacrificed for." She made a steeple of her fingers and touched them to her chin. "I hope you can understand, Amy, and will someday be able to forgive me."

Amy slipped to the floor at her mother's feet. "There is nothing to forgive. You are my mother and I will always love you." She paused. "In all honesty, there was a time when I hated you for having left us, but Aunt Charlotte helped me to understand."

"Then she has my undying gratitude." She pushed Amy's hair back from her forehead. "But

238

come, enough of this serious talk. We must plan what to wear when we go downstairs." She looked uncertainly at the picnic hamper that Amy had placed on the floor when she came in. "I hope you brought something to wear besides the riding costume you have on."

Amy laughed. "I have a few gowns. The picnic hamper was the only means I had of bringing them without Jason getting word that I had run away. I must warn you. There is no doubt in my mind that he will follow after me in a few days, and he may be inclined toward violence. I fear I have sorely tried his patience more than once."

"Jason is a fool if he doesn't marry you. He's like your father, in some respects: stubborn, moralistic, and always completely sure that he knows what's best for everyone. Just don't give up too easily if you want him. He was a fine boy and has, I'm sure, grown into a finer man."

She stood up and fluffed her hair. "But come. We don't have a great deal of time before high tea. After the performance we will have a late dinner, then stay up until all hours of the morning to talk about the theatre and the play. I hope you won't find it boring."

She picked up a gown from the floor, eyed it thoughtfully, and threw it on the bed in disgust. "I'll expect you to stay the night with me and in the morning we can see to a room for you." She hesitated. "I—I hope you are not without funds.

239

While I manage quite well for myself, it would be somewhat difficult . . ."

"It's all right. I have enough money to last for a time." She looked around. "Would you like me to hang up some of these gowns and wrappers?"

Emily threw her head back and laughed. "If it would please you, my dear, but you will find I'm not a very orderly person."

Amy smiled apologetically. "I thought it would give us more room to move around."

An hour later the room was tidy, if not spotless, and the women were dressed to go downstairs. Amy had chosen a simple gown but her mother insisted she wear her most seductively cut dress of apricot satin, saying that it would be more in keeping with what the other women would be wearing. Amy reluctantly agreed.

As they left the room and started along the gallery leading to the stairs, Count Borelli came bounding toward them nearly out of breath. A strange excitement glinted in his eyes as he grasped Amy's arm.

"It's your guardian, Lord Winford. He's downstairs with the innkeeper at this moment inquiring for your mother's room."

Amy's hands flew to her face. "Oh, dear. So soon? I knew he would come but I thought . . ." She looked at her mother with concern. "It's too soon. I need more time."

Emily nodded. "Yes. Perhaps it would be best if I talk to him alone."

Amy shook her head. "He is sure to be in a terrible rage. I can't let you bear the brunt of his anger."

"Don't be silly, Amy. He is not going to harm me. I am, after all, your mother." She reached out to Amy and took her hands in her own. "I *am* your mother, Amy. Please, just this once, let me act the part," she pleaded.

Amy nodded and brushed her mother's cheek with a kiss. Count Borelli took her by the arm. "Then you can't remain here. Come, I'll take you to my room on the floor below, but we must hurry or he will be here before we make the stairs."

CHAPTER FIFTEEN

Amy hesitated for little more than a glance at her mother, then let herself be propelled down the stairs. Count Borelli's bedchamber was considerably more luxurious than her mother's room, though not much larger. Amy was gratified to see the bed, neatly made, was spread with a cover and there was little evidence of his having slept there. She relaxed until he closed the door and she heard the key grate as he turned it.

"So that we won't be surprised," he smiled disarmingly. "Won't you sit down?" He motioned to the bed. She chose a straight-backed chair by the door. There was a glint of humor in his eyes. "You look most uncomfortable, my lady. Won't you join me in a glass of wine?"

"Thank you, no. While I sincerely appreciate your kindness, I do not expect to be here for more than a very few minutes. I—I'm sure you must realize it is most unseemly for me to be alone with you in your bedchamber, and I would not want it to appear as a social occasion."

The count threw back his head and laughed. "My dear lady. Judging from your past performances, I would not have thought you overly concerned about appearances. Indeed, rumor has it that you are your mother's daughter in more than looks."

Amy bristled. "I'm sure I have no idea what you mean, sir!"

He came to stand beside her and picked up her hand, holding it so firmly that she could not pull away. "Really, you are even a better actress than most people realize. It is a well-known fact that every dasher in the beau monde is after you. You have been seen on the arm of a number of young bucks, including Beau Brummell himself. That is until your guardian whisked you away to the country." His tone grew nasty. "I'll wager he takes his services as a guardian out in trade."

Amy stood up quickly and brought her free hand against his face in a resounding slap. "You have a filthy mouth, Count Borelli, and you would do well to keep it closed."

He grabbed her roughly, pinioning her arms until she gasped with pain. "Don't play games with me, my lady. You like to play hard to get like your mother does but what you need is a real man to teach you some new rules." He bent his face over hers and covered her skin with hot, wet kisses. "That's right, struggle. It makes it all the more interesting."

"Jason will kill you when he learns of this."

He laughed. "If his lordship were truly concerned about you he would be here by now. Perhaps he prefers a woman of experience like your mother." Amy kicked him on the leg and though he groaned in pain, he didn't release his hold on her. Clutching her wrists in one hand behind her back, he grasped the top of her gown in his other hand and was about to rip it down when Amy screamed. He tried to cover her mouth but she bit his hand and screamed again.

Seconds later there was a pounding on the door and Jason's deep voice demanded that they open it. The count swore as he fought to control his rage, then slowly loosened his grip.

As the pounding grew louder Amy tore herself free and ran to the other side of the room, adjusting her gown and smoothing her hair. With her hand on the doorknob it suddenly occurred to her that she had put Jason in the position of having to defend her honor. If indeed Jason had to rescue her from an indiscretion, it was one thing, but to be rescued from an attack would surely mean that Jason would be obliged to call him out. She couldn't let that happen.

She drew a deep breath and tried to assume a look of cool hauteur as she turned the key and opened the door. "So . . . you have come chasing after me again, my lord. Really, isn't this carrying it a bit too far?"

His expression showed more concern for her safety than she had expected. He reached for her shoulders. "A—are you all right? We heard you scream. If he has harmed you I'll have him drawn and quartered."

Amy struggled to keep her voice light. "Harmed me? What on earth do you mean, Jason? He simply gave me a chance to gather my wits before having to face you."

"I—but you screamed." He looked confused. "I thought . . ."

"Goodness, how amusing. It was only a wee mouse that scurried across the floor and tried to climb my skirt. It surprised me, that's all."

Behind Jason's back Emily Concord smiled, but quickly covered her mouth with her hand. "Come, the two of you. Why don't we go to my room where we can talk in private without attracting an audience. I see a few doors beginning to open. I'm sure Count Borelli will excuse us." She leaned inside to look at him. "I'm sure we all appreciate what you have tried to do for Amy, Count Borelli. Be assured, I won't forget it." Amy recognized the

245

veiled threat in her mother's voice and almost felt sorry for the man.

The three of them climbed the stairs to Emily's room and were somewhat awkward in each other's company until Emily broke the silence.

"Lord Jason and I have spoken at considerable length, Amy, and we both feel better for having aired our views. I know he will explain everything later. Suffice it to say that much as I regret having to send you away so soon, we both feel it prudent for you to return to Winford Farms without delay." She looked at Jason with respect and understanding. "Another time we will arrange for a more leisurely visit. Now, if you will excuse me for a few minutes, there is something of importance to which I must attend."

Amy was not quite ready to be left alone with Jason. True, his concern and anger seemed to have diminished, but there were times when his quiet was more to be feared than his temper. She stood with her back against the wall, hands pressed against the dingy wallpaper, afraid, almost, to breathe.

Jason laced his fingers together behind his back and strode to the windows, turning twice as if to say something, then apparently changing his mind. He was obviously hurting inside but didn't know what to do about it.

Amy's heart went out to him and she walked over to stand behind him. "It's not going to work,

Jason . . . my going back with you. I could not stay there the way things are, and I do not wish to go into seclusion in London." Her voice caught and she had to clear her throat. "I want you to know that I wish you and Lady Elizabeth all the happiness in the world. I—I'll always be grateful for everything you have done for me."

He turned slowly, a fire blazing deep in his eyes. "I don't want your gratitude, Amy."

She saw he was trying to control himself. His mouth was set in a thin line; a nerve jumped at the corner of his eye. She shook her head, fighting back the tears. "Gratitude is all I have left to give. What more do you want from me, Jason?"

"Everything. But most of all, your love."

"Oh, Jason, don't do this to me." The words were torn from her heart. "Don't make me bare my soul. You know I love you and always will no matter whom you choose to make your wife."

"I choose you, Amy, my beloved. I chose you many months ago but was afraid to admit it. I'm asking you to be my wife."

Tears matted her lashes and spilled onto her cheeks as she searched his face. "And what about Lady Elizabeth? She told me of your betrothal."

He placed his hands on each side of her face and smoothed away her tears with his thumbs. "There was no betrothal, Amy, only a faint understanding on the part of our families that they were both agreeable to the union. Elizabeth and

I have never gone beyond the bounds of friendship. I admit that she has suggested a time or two that we could please our families by linking our two names, but I have never encouraged her."

"And what of your family? How will they accept our betrothal?"

"I'm sure my father will be pleased. Aunt Charlotte certainly finds the idea appealing. As for your mother, it was she who gave me the courage to approach you now instead of waiting for my father to return. But I tell you this . . . if they were all against us, I would still want you to be my wife."

Amy was suddenly afraid that she could not live up to his expectations. She began to tremble and he folded her in his arms, so close that she could hear his breath as he spoke.

"You are trembling. Surely you are not afraid of me, Amy. I would die rather than hurt you."

"No, my lord," she whispered. "I only fear that I will disappoint you. I am totally inexperienced in the ways of the bed."

He chuckled. "Believe me, my darling, you have no need to feel concern. We will give each other more pleasure than either of us can comprehend. In truth your kiss alone has moved me more than anything in the world has done before."

She smiled up into his eyes and reached for his head, pulling it down to her level. They kissed gently, too moved by love to court the danger of passion. She was still resting in his arms when her mother returned. The sight of them brought a tender smile to Emily Concord's lips.

Danielle Steel
SUMMER'S END

author of *The Promise*
and *Season of Passion*

As the wife of handsome, successful, international lawyer Marc Edouard Duras, Deanna had a beautiful home, diamonds and elegant dinners. But her husband was traveling between the glamorous capitals of the business world, and all summer Deanna would be alone. Until Ben Thomas found her—and laughter and love took them both by surprise.

A Dell Book $2.50

At your local bookstore or use this handy coupon for ordering:

Dell

DELL BOOKS   SUMMER'S END $2.50 (18418-5)
P.O. BOX 1000, PINEBROOK, N.J. 07058

Please send me the above title. I am enclosing $ _____
(please add 75¢ per copy to cover postage and handling). Send check or money order—no cash or C.O.D.'s. Please allow up to 8 weeks for shipment.

Mr/Mrs/Miss _____

Address _____

City _____ State/Zip _____

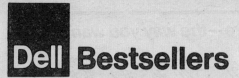

Hester

The Roundtree Women

BOOK III

by Margaret Lewerth

The third volume in the tumultuous 4-part saga, HESTER joins **The Roundtree Women, Book I** and **Claude: The Roundtree Women, Book II** in recounting the triumphs and tragedies of the Roundtree family. Especially the Roundtree women, who defied convention and risked scandal—in the name of love! A deathless passion drew Hester Brady into the Roundtree circle. One man claimed her, but another enflamed her passions and possessed her fiery soul!

A Dell Book $2.50

In this first stirring novel in a 4-part series, you will meet: Henrietta, the exotic New Orleans beauty who became the matriarch of the Roundtree clan; Lowell, the fiance of Duncan Phelps, whose spirit runs wild with secret shame about to explode! And Ariel, Lowell's Paris bred cousin and a restless sophisticate, her destiny calls her back to her ancestral land—and Duncan Phelps. They are proud. Sensual. Commanding. It is in their blood to take what they have to have.

A DELL BOOK $2.50
(17594-1)

Margaret   Lewerth

The Roundtree Women

Book 1

**The Roundtree Women love
only once. Forevermore!**